Henry Pearson was born in 2004 and grew up in Bournemouth in a family of six, with three siblings and two dogs. He attended St Peter's secondary school and is currently studying at Keble College, Oxford. His passion for creating worlds of his own comes from his family's adventure-style holidays and his love of all things geek. 'Bonds' is his first novel which he wrote during the second COVID-19 lockdown.

For Suzie

Henry T. G. Pearson

BONDS

AUSTIN MACAULEY PUBLISHERS™

LONDON • CAMBRIDGE • NEW YORK • SHARJAH

A CIP catalogue record for this title is available from the British Library.

ISBN 9781398472563 (Paperback)
ISBN 9781398472570 (ePub e-book)

www.austinmacauley.com

First Published 2022
Austin Macauley Publishers Ltd®
1 Canada Square
Canary Wharf
London
E14 5AA

The first and most obvious person that I must thank is my mum without whom this dream of mine would never have come to fruition. She's the captain of the Pearson family ship and pretty much everything would go kaput if she was not there to keep everyone in check!

The next thank you goes to the rest of my family: Dad, Rosa, Ed and Louisa who are supportive of me no matter how much of a mistake I make. Although when I do make a mistake, they're unlikely to let me forget it. I must also thank my friends who keep me entertained and motivated, and are always there when I need help and advice, as well as all the teachers that have influenced my writing over the years.

Table of Contents

Art Part 1

Long golden rays lay suspended on the ocean. The water was still, nothing but the slightest of ripples disturbed its surface and the great ship glided through the deep blue, piercing the serenity of the bleak landscape.

Art left the top deck to begin his duties – starting with mopping the floor. The immense wooden panels that made up the ship were old and worn, some cracked and others worked smooth by crewmates that moved here and there, always doing something to keep the vessel afloat and on the right course. The sails were furled and unfurled when necessary and the giant masts were rotated to face the wind that arduously pushed the boat towards the bleak horizon.

The chaos was why Art joined the crew, he revelled in it. Everyone had something to do, a job to keep everything working, even Art. Although mopping wasn't the most important job, that right was reserved for the captain. He was a huge man, skin like tanned leather but with the eyes of a hawk, always watching. His sinuous muscles pulled his shirt taught giving him a hulking appearance. Despite his looks, however, he was a kind man, a man that took care to make sure his crew were as a happy as possible and that his ship was in top condition. The latter of which was proving tough for Art as he was the one cleaning the great boughs and planks that were masterfully latticed together to form the ship's skeleton. It was the captain that had rescued Art and guided him on a safer path.

"Keep cleaning, Art, it looks good, let's make it better," the captain shouted with a wink.

Art smiled back and continued mopping beneath the hot sun whilst the wind blew past his face, caressing his cheek and wiping the sweat from his brow. He was grateful for its cooling touch.

Hours trudged by on the open sea, not a sight of the unfortunate destination of the voyage. Art had heard tales of the place but he suspected them to be mere rumours and folk tales, no place could be that dangerous or steeped in mystery. Many a sailor had lost their life on its shores, few had reached inland, none had returned. Art tried to avoid the sense of impending doom but it was always in the corner of his mind, nagging at him to ask the captain the reason for travelling to such a place. But none of the crew knew, they just followed the captain like a hive mind with no thought of their own safety.

Art was less sure. He wasn't going to run head first somewhere he may not return, even if he did trust the captain with his life. He was worth more than that; he wasn't going to become cannon fodder. Anger crept into his stomach, leaching away at the freedom he had felt only moments before. *Even my old life is better than no life at all.*

He slowly let the anger disperse, his mind reeling back in to focus on the task at hand and not get too distracted with thoughts of the future.

"Land ho," yelled a voice from the crow's nest.

Art leaped into action, pulling on ropes to furl up the sails and helping drop anchor. The chaos stole his mind away from thought once again as he lost himself to the rhythmic heave of the chains.

As they closed in on the shore, they dropped anchor and waited for orders, all keen to leave the ship but all fearing the island they were about to set foot upon. The whole bay was still, eerily so and Art felt uneasy at the sight of the looming mountain and gloomy forest but he remained on deck waiting for what the captain had to say.

The man cleared his throat, made to speak but didn't. It was like the words were trapped in the back of his throat. Eventually he did make a noise but it wasn't words, it was a gargle followed by blood and one last outward breath. The giant of a man collapsed on the deck in a heap of his own blood with two arrows sticking out of his back.

The ship erupted with movement, the crew all looking to run and escape before whatever had killed their captain found them. Art was terrified, his heart pounding, his mind racing to find a way to survive. His legs began to take him towards a rowing boat with lightning speed. Just as he reached it, the ropes were cut and the small vessel and eight men went crashing towards the turquoise water, leaving him standing helpless at the side of the ship. The small boat raced off towards the shore but Art didn't look for long, as screams drew his eyes to the quarter-deck where steel was clashing against steel, the crew seemed to fighting some indigenous tribe that had swarmed the ship. There were men and women clothed in thick hides and cloth, armed with swords and pole arms, fighting like an organised army, far more militarily capable than the sea-scum that were trying desperately to escape this deadly foe.

Art ran in the opposite direction, taking a glance towards the rowing boat that was now engulfed in flames and dived into the sea below.

He landed with a splash, gathered himself and swam towards the hull, grabbing hold of it and moving his way around the ship towards the rudder in an attempt to hide himself from the indigenous people. Others were jumping into the water but they swam for shore and were picked off one by one, skewered like fish by javelins. Art knew he was counting his breaths, they would not take prisoners. He would not survive this.

Luke Part 1

"Luke, please, hurry. You'll be late for the city council!"

"Do I have to go, Mother? I'd much prefer to stay at home. Wouldn't Father prefer it if he went alone?"

"He asked for you personally. Don't forget some of the most influential people in the city will be there and I would love to show you off to them, possibly find you a wife with a rich family. Your father would like that very much and so would I, now get ready to go out. I've picked out a marvellous gown for you to wear."

Luke's father was a cloth merchant, a family trade passed down over a couple hundred years and Luke was keen to keep it going. The young boy often spent time thinking about how he would improve the business and become rich enough to sail the world and dine with kings. He had ambitions to become a king himself but he kept those to himself in fear of humiliation. However, he was young, only ten years old, so he knew he would have to wait a long time to inherit his father's wealth and business but he was canny, quick-witted for his age and often snuck into meetings and conferences his father held with the other wealthy merchants in the city. The boy was like a criminal, often creeping around and snooping through his father's belongings but he was sure never to be caught as he was certain that if his father found him out, he would not pass down the family business.

Luke, slowly trudged upstairs, lost in thought. As he entered the room, he was welcomed with the familiar scent of honey and cinnamon; his housemaids were just finishing dusting the many book-laden shelves in his room but quickly dispersed as he walked in. The room was cold but homely, stacked with many oddities that he had been given by his parents and their wealthy friends in one corner sat a desk, accompanied by a small but beautifully designed candelabra. That small space was where he spent most of his time, studying and planning for everything that he would do when he grew up. For hours, he would scratch away at his desk with quill and ink, creating elaborate plans for his future, every business deal, every voyage and purchase. He had it all worked out, no detail spared. Neither his parents knew that he had such an intimate understanding of the world around him and he tried his best to hide it, unsure if he would meet their high expectations and desperate not to raise them further.

As he made his way to his closet, a servant walked in and brought with him the garments his mother had prepared. They were a dull brown, as was the fashion, and were coated with patterns, almost too much to take in. Luke knew that they would be well received by the gentlemen he would be meeting today but he felt foolish in them like a pet in an outfit, not able to move freely. The servant carefully placed the final bow, did up the boy's laces and left him, standing awkwardly in front of the mirror his mother had bought from India. He looked himself up and down, pushed his hands through his sun-bleached blonde hair, rearranged it and walked back downstairs to his mother, her face beaming at her creation but

Luke didn't know whether she was pleased with him or the robes.

"Oh my. Don't you look good!"

He blushed and opened his mouth about to say thank you before he was interrupted.

"Yes, I really have done well this time, haven't I, darling?" she said, directing the question to her husband who had just entered the room, also dressed in fine clothing.

"Like always, my dear," he replied with a kiss.

Both Luke and his mother were surprised at this show of affection, the tall boisterous man rarely showed emotion to anyone, not even his family, so having him openly kiss his wife was very uncomfortable for everyone who witnessed it. The cold, often heartless merchant stood motionless as though he too was surprised at his actions. Then, after a few awkward seconds he smiled a crooked smile like his face had forgotten how to. The man's cheeks began to twitch, an involuntary reaction to acting so differently to from his usual demeanour. Luke stepped forwards, hoping to save his father from any more embarrassment and went to open the door.

The two men silently made their way outside, walking hastily, readying themselves for the council meeting, both sweating and puffing their cheeks out in worry as the pair weren't very fond of socialising beyond business. They were undeniably similar, yet Luke wanted to be different to the icy, calculating merchant he walked beside, he wanted to be able to show who he really was, his real emotions, not the synthetic personality that his father was so used to using.

When will we get there? Luke was desperate to get this overemphasised event over and done with so he could go back to his quiet room and his maple desk. The boy turned his

17

attention to his father who met his hazel eyes with a silent judgement. The man made to speak but stopped himself and continued walking forwards, avoiding his son's love-seeking gaze.

The streets were clean in this part of London, no poverty or sadness, just emptiness. The houses were all freshly painted, windows immaculate but there was nothing human about it. The air was unpolluted, stripped from the impurities of the lower class, yet it had no character, even the wind was silent as it drifted past the lamps and fences. There were people but they kept to themselves, fearful of being mugged or catching a disease. It was like they had been distanced from the poor for so long that they feared them, even in the richest neighbourhoods in the city. The poor were an unspoken curse and Luke liked it that way.

Luke was watching the clouds, admiring their freedom and serenity in a world that was clogged with impurity, uncertainty and fear. They just drifted, compliant with where the wind took them. But as Luke turned his head, he noticed that the clouds were suddenly turning from snow white to ashen, black and menacing, despite the weather being unchanged.

"My God, Luke, look," shouted his father, his voice cracking.

Luke looked to where he was pointing and saw giant amber spires of flame, climbing higher into the sky with every gust of wind. The clouds Luke had noticed weren't clouds at all, they were smoke, billowing from the inferno across the river, infiltrating the sky like a swarm of ravens. The fire was spreading fast, engulfing London in flame, devouring the city and turning it to ash.

Screams began to float Luke's way muffled by the roar of the fire. His father stopped walking and watched the flames crawl their way towards the docks by the Thames.

"My ships…" The man began to sprint towards the docks, ripping his suit and throwing his briefcase to the floor. Luke ran after him.

"Father! Save the ships!" The boy knew that if the ships burned, all his plans for his future would be in jeopardy. "Quick, Father, hurry or they'll be burned!"

The man turned back towards his son, nodded and ran off once more, desperate to save his life's work. Luke still continued after him, hoping to help salvage what he could but no matter how fast either of them could run the blaze was faster and by the time they had reached the bridge, the docks had ignited and along with it the family business. Luke's father however did not stop and continued towards the burning dockyards. Luke just stopped and sobbed. *My whole future, now ashes. What can I do now? I'll have to build the business back up again, break my back like the poor.*

The boy wiped his eyes and ran off after his father, hoping to save him from trying to recover what was already lost.

The streets were packed with civilians running to and fro, some running away from the fire, others running towards it with buckets of water and sand. There was a family on their knees crying, faces caked in soot and ash, their tears streaking through the grime and dripping off their chin. *They've lost everything. I've lost everything.*

Luke pushed his way past the hordes of people trying to spot his father but he could not see him amidst the chaos. He could hardly breathe, the smoke suffocating him whilst the crowds squashed him, too busy in their own escape to notice the small boy. It seemed like the whole of London had been crammed into one dirty street, shouts and screams and sobs adding to the cacophony, all overcome by the searing roar of the fire. The king's guard had even been dispatched to help try and appease the flames, their red uniforms matching the red of the inferno. It seemed pointless trying to put it out, it was enormous, it's smoke, a black cloak over the city, and it would take an army to even attempt such a monumental task.

Luke stopped and watched as the crowd bustled, all kinds of people trapped by the blaze. There were vagrants, families, bakers, even merchants like Luke's father. Among the hordes were ragged men, all carrying potato sacs, they had drawn Luke's eye as they moved differently to the rest of the crowd, they had a purpose, they knew exactly what to do and seemed unfazed by the fire, almost pleased by it. Each one had a crooked sneer on their face, some even laughing, a stark difference to everyone else who were running in desperate panic.

Just as Luke jumped back into the crowd to find his father, he caught the eye of one of the men, this one tall, wearing a maritime jacket, a cutlass sheathed in his belt. The man came straight for Luke, a gleam in his eye. Luke turned, frantically pushing people so that he could slip past but there were too many and before long, the man was behind him, sac clasped firmly in each hand.

The last thing Luke remembered was the sac being violently pulled over his head.

Art Part 2

Art's heart pounded in his chest. He held desperately to the hull, his legs being pulled away by the ocean current. Thoughts about letting go swarmed his mind, knowing that trying to survive would only prolong his torture but instead he hung on, hoping that the indigenous wouldn't notice him and he could somehow escape this dreadful situation.

The waves lashed against the hull, rocking the boat and testing Art's grip. The commotion on deck had stopped; all the remaining crew had been slaughtered. So, far it seemed like Art had not been noticed as the tribe appeared to be moving away from the boat and into the darkness of the island's thick undergrowth that leaked a dark, menacing fog. Every breath Art took was shallow and cold, his best attempt to keep quiet and out of the radar of the deadly tribesmen but as time dragged on, he felt his grip deteriorate. His hands began to ache, a deep tearing pain that was quickly becoming too much to bear. After holding on for another few desperate seconds, Art's hands finally conceded to the agony, leaving the current free to drag him out to open water. He frantically swam against the pull of the sea, careful not to cause too much of a ruckus and attract unwanted attention. But he was no match for the ocean and began to drift out away from the ship.

In a fret of panic, Art decided not to move to just let the current take him. *Maybe they'll mistake me for a body.* Art knew his life was relying on thin ice but all he could do was hope.

As he floated away, he spied what looked like the chieftain of the tribe grabbing a torch and setting it down upon the ship, letting the flames dance up the mast and across the deck. Art couldn't help but watch. It was stunning. The amber glow of the fire was enticing, drawing him in until he couldn't take his eyes away. The crimson spikes spread across the whole ship, engulfing it. Art laid his head back, a deep fatigue setting in, stealing him away from the conscious world.

His tired eyes opened wearily and took a deep breath in shock, the current had dragged him to shore, his aching body snagging on a small outcropping of rock. He checked his body over, a precaution in case he was dreaming or had been killed in his sleep, neither was true. The island seemed calmer, the waves less violent, the sun less burning, however, the thick black smoke escaping the jungle was still there, a wordless evil that made Art shiver. There was no sign of the indigenous, save for a few footprints in the white sand, some stained with thick red blood. Art looked to the ship but it was far in the distance, almost at the other end of the island, its splendour reduced to ash and embers. Art shed a tear, not for the ship but for what it stood for, it was his freedom, his escape. Then he remembered the captain, the man who had saved him from the dirt of London's streets, also humbled by the tribe.

The sun was beginning to set, its last few golden rays bouncing off the surface of the water. Art began to realise that he was in great danger alone on the island, he was lucky to have evaded the tribe but spending a night here would almost certainly spell his demise. He sat, just thinking for a few moments, planning his survival in this treacherous place until a voice, quiet and harsh, like the hiss of a snake scratched at his head.

"You should be dead. No one gets past the hunters."

The voice seemed empty, emotionless. It was like only he could hear it, every syllable reverberating in his head like a whisper but he wasn't hearing it. He was feeling it.

Art was ridden with fear, his stomach tightened and his breath grew short, his lips and mouth suddenly became dry. His movements became erratic and he paced up and down the beach, as he did so, the voice spoke again.

"If I were you, I'd get off the beach, it's too open. They'll find you."

The last sentence sent a chill cascading down Art's spine. *Who will find me? The hunters or…or worse?* He tried not to think too hard on it and instead began to slowly step towards the jungle. Art could feel his heart racing and heard every grain of sand crunch as he stepped, he was hyper alert on edge with fear.

"Quick, get into the forest or they'll see you!"

The harsh whisper made him jump, making his hands shake feverishly as a result. He picked up the pace, taking heed of the mysterious voice's warning, hoping that it was not a trap. The dark fog seemed to envelope him as he took a cautious step into the undergrowth, however, the fog only outlined the jungle as though it too feared to venture further. The thought made Art even more terrified, he prayed that he wouldn't come across the monsters said to dwell in this hell but he was not a religious man and held little hope for his survival.

The jungle was dark, the thick foliage from the trees blocking most of the sunlight from lighting the ground, making the place ominous and gothic like a dungeon deep below the fortified walls of a castle. The wind drifted slowly through the trunks, whistling as it went and the leaves of the trees and bushes joined in with the song but it was not like any bird song. This song was dark and dreary, more akin to a funeral chant and it began to drive Art crazy. Every crackle of a leaf, he would jump and stand still, petrified, frantically looking around for danger. His nerves were stretched thin.

The forest seemed impenetrable from Art's vantage point, there were no paths, hardly any light and the trees were huge, towering above his head higher than any building he had ever seen. He would check them regularly, watching their branches for the predators that were never there. But he felt watched, hunted; a mouse in a trap. He kept his eyes facing forwards, searching for a spot to sleep for the night, however, he didn't even know if it was night, the light had not faded but he was exhausted, crippled by the constant fear that had crept into him.

Finally, after what seemed like a lifetime of walking aimlessly through the undergrowth, Art found a small flat open grove where he could rest. He checked the perimeter countless times for anything remotely harmful be it plant or animal and when he finally felt safe enough, he collapsed against a thick winding trunk. He was asleep almost instantly, his sheer exhaustion overpowering his fear sending him into a deep slumber that left him helpless, ripe for the picking.

Art woke peacefully, surprised that he had slept undisturbed and grateful that he had not been eaten. He stood up slowly, his muscles and bones aching and his joints cracking in protest. He stretched out his arms, yawned and began planning what to do with the day ahead of him, although he was still unsure of the time as the forest remained a fortress of darkness.

"You were lucky they didn't get you," the voice whispered, sounding irritated.

Art considered replying, wondered if it would hear him. He decided not to, conceding to his fear and caution but the voice continued to speak.

"There's a storm coming soon and with the storm comes much more than just thunder and lightning."

Art gulped, an involuntary action. He didn't know what to do, he tried desperately not to ask more but his curiosity and anxiety egged him on.

"What should I do?" he squeaked.

"Hide."

The word was hissed violently, adding to its severity. Art froze, once again stranded by fear. He was struck with a host of different emotions, fear for his safety, anger at the voice and sadness at the constant affirmation that he would not make it off this island. He cried, once again reminiscing over the death of the captain. *He would know what to do; he would've already got us off this retched island.* Art fell to his knees, his cries becoming violent sobs that shook his whole body. He felt so alone, so lost. His only hope was tied to one word.

Hide.

Luke Part 2

Luke had been on the boat for weeks, chained to a wall along with around 30 other boys, some younger, some older. They had finally gotten used to the slow sway of the ship but for the first couple days they were all seasick and homesick, most of them crying at some point, fearing for their lives. The first day was the worst, two boys had died of their injuries and another two had died of heat stroke, dehydration and panic; it was carnage.

It was now night, the claustrophobic cabin they had been stored in was dark and stank of faeces and urine as well as sweat and the metallic twang of blood, Luke didn't think he'd ever get used to the smell, it was putrid. Exhausted, he laid his head against the plank he was chained to and peered through a small gap between two planks. There was no sight of land, there hadn't been for a long time, there was just an inescapable expanse of azure that stretched as far as Luke could see. The stars were reflected on the water, making it look like they were flying, soaring through the sky with nothing but the bleak black sky to keep them company. Luke began to doze off but was disturbed by the rattle of chains and a slight groan that came from the other side of the prison. The youngest boy, only around eight was moving in his sleep, a nightmare, Luke assumed, because no one could dream happily in such conditions.

The morning came too quickly, the sun rising to break the peace of night and with it came the shouts of the crew and captain unfurling the mast and beginning the day's work. All the boys were awake at this point, although many had deep purple circles around their eyes. Footsteps could be heard coming down the stairs from the top deck and as an involuntary response all the boys stood up, trained by the countless beatings they'd received from not doing what they were told or what was expected. But after weeks of practice, the boys knew the drill. Luke rubbed his eyes and stared through the iron bars, waiting for Kastas, their appointed carer, to bring them their morning morsels. Instead, however, the captain appeared, his gruesome smile sending a spike of fear through Luke. He hadn't seen those gold and rotten teeth since the day he was taken and every day since then, Luke had dreamed of killing this scoundrel, lopping his head off with his own cutlass. The man seemed to feel the tension and held Luke's eye contact for an uncomfortable amount of time before opening his mouth to speak.

"We're close to Tortuga boys, only a couple more days until your maiden voyage is over and might I say what a good job you've done so far."

The man was speaking to them with a harshly sarcastic tone and every time he moved, the boys flinched.

"At Tortuga, you'll be sold and grab me and m'crew a mighty fine bounty, so of course to increase our chances of selling you lot, me and the boys have decided to let you up on deck today and if you're lucky we'll let you feast with us."

The boys all licked their lips.

"But, if any one of you misbehaves, well, let's just say you won't be makin' it off this here boat. Am I understood?"

The question was followed by a wave of nods from the boys who suddenly seemed much more awake like the thought of being freed from this cabin had lit a fire in them. Luke knew that the Captain was planning something malicious, his cunning smile hiding his true intent. *These uneducated poor have no idea what the pirates are like, they're acting like retched hounds, scavenging for any hope they can get. I'm different, I see through the deception, through that criminal's lies.* Luke snarled slightly at the thought of once again being trapped by the pirates, which shocked him. *I don't act like that, I'm civilised or am I just as bad as these dogs?* He looked around, eyeing each boy intently and they all had a gleam in their eyes, a slither of hope. Despite spending what Luke assumed was around two months chained up with these boys, he hardly knew any of their names. He had initially isolated himself on purpose, not wanting to associate with those less privileged than himself but eventually it became a habit, they too making sure not to talk to him, spooked by his determination to remain alone. It only made things harder for him and deep down he knew it but he didn't want to admit fault, not even to himself.

The small group was led out of the cage they had been cooped up in and made their way up the stairs to the deck. The sun was unbearable for their eyes which had become accustomed to the gloom of the prison. It's golden rays pierced the back of Luke's eyes, forcing him to cover them with his grimy hands. But the warmth it provided was glorious, feeding Luke's aching bones and tired muscles with a vigorous energy that he hadn't felt for a very long time. The other boys also seemed to feel the sun's power and collectively they began to move more fluidly, less like a mindless hoard and more like individuals, as though they had regained their identity. Luke hadn't seen the deck before and was surprised at how clean it was, the sun glinting off the slightly damp wooden panels, it seemed uncharacteristic of pirate scum to keep something so clean. Subconsciously, Luke was jealous; the boys had been stored in almost inhabitable conditions whilst the pirates revelled in their squalor. *I am a merchant's son and have been packed into a cage like an animal while these criminals have been living like royalty.* Anger slowly poisoned Luke's thoughts but he managed to control it, not wanting to be slaughtered out at sea. The marvel of the deck, however, was tainted by the crew that lived on it. All of the men were ragged and untamed, unruly beasts, their skin a canvas of scars, their clothes ripped and hanging loose over their sinuous bodies. Luke then looked at himself. *I'm worse than them, what have they made me into?*

The captain smiled at his crew, an evil sneer and then began to tell each one of them what to do. It was impressive to watch, every single member had a job and was so practiced at it that the whole routine was immaculate. There were men tugging on ropes, others tying ropes to the rails and a small, primate-like pirate rapidly ascending the mast all the way to the crow's nest.

"You see, boys, eventually you'll be doing that as well, maybe not as perfectly as my ragged bunch but I'm sure you'll make fine crew members."

The captain shouted the last part, making the rest of the pirates laugh and adding to Luke's suspicions. The tall man was in front of the wheel, his back turned on the boys that had all huddled at the back of the ship just watching silently, too afraid to speak out of turn. Luke was thankful to be outside, the wind blowing all rotten scents out to sea. This was the closest to luxury he had felt since being kidnapped, although it was far from what he was used to at home.

Luke was stuck at the back of the huddle, sandwiched between two of the older boys but glad to be out of the captain's line of sight. Then the boys started moving and pointing out to sea gasping with relief. Out on the horizon was an island, barely visible. Luke breathed heavily, his palms grew sweaty and his elbow began to itch. To him, this was the only way off the boat but he wasn't sure if what they were ploughing towards would be better or worse. The sails were unfurled further, snagged by the wind that pushed them smoothly through the water, whether Luke liked it or not, they were at full speed and heading straight for land.

The day moved slowly, it was like the sun was enjoying Luke's torture and was forcing him to endure its barrage of heat. All 30 of the boys were feeling the wrath of the climate and it seemed the crew were too, although they had access to a rusty ladle in a barrel of fresh water. Luke licked his lips, watching one of the leathery men drink a large spoonful, his mouth was dry, his lips crusted. Eventually the captain himself went to wet his pallet, he grabbed the ladle, lifted it to the boys, still smiling and took a long gulp, he wanted the boys to feel miserable, he wanted to break their spirits. Luke looked away, hatred boiling inside him. The captain made his way back up the deck, water dripping down his chin but as he walked past the boys, one of them vomited onto his shoes. The smile was wiped off his face in an instant, replaced by a hideous grimace. The boy looked up at him, terror in his eyes and apologised.

"That's okay, my boy, we all make mistakes," the captain whispered, and in a flash his cutlass was unsheathed and was embedded into the boy's stomach. His smile was back. The small boy collapsed onto the ground, his blood spreading across the deck. They all fell silent.

It was Kastas who eventually brought the boys something to drink; he trudged up the stairs to the upper deck holding a silver bucket full of water, carefully stepping over the dead body. He seemed to be the only pirate with any kindness, although Luke suspected it was only because he pitied the boys for what they would be put through. He was older than most the other men, his tanned face heavy with wrinkles and his hands shook as he offered Luke a ladle. As Luke drank he looked into the old man's eyes, they were slightly pale and told a thousand stories of pain and torment, he looked away and offered the next boy a drink but Luke was still watching his eyes, their sadness gripping him, Luke wanted to know more.

The day began to draw to a close and just as the sun began to set, the captain turned and faced the boys. His eyes drifted over the body that lay twitching on the ground.

"Kastas would you bring a mop up here and clean up this…accident."

"Aye, captain, I'll be up right away!"

"Anyways, it seems we have all made it to the end of the day, well, most of us. And, as a man of my word, I shall let the rest of you dine with the crew tonight, a parting gift of sorts. So, if you'd all follow me to the lower deck."

The boys went without a word, salivating as they sat down. The pirates had begun to bring out all kinds of exotic foods from inside one of the cabins. There were fruits and vegetables, as well as a variety of meats and cheeses; it was as fancy as a royal feast, despite the fact that those eating were criminals. The boys were kindly asked to wait until the crew had finished and not one of them complained. The food was phenomenal, better tasting than anything Luke had ever eaten before and a stark difference to what he'd been fed previously on the ship. Even after the boys had tucked in, there was plenty spare. Luke had stuffed himself, expecting that this would be his last meal for a while and it appeared some of the other boys had the same suspicions as a couple of them had run to the side of the boat to vomit, their stomachs not used to eating so much, especially after being fed scraps for over two months. That night they slept on the deck and watched the stars, all of them sleeping soundly.

Luke slept through the entire night which was heaven for his sore bones, although he still had to sleep on the hard wooden planks. The peace was interrupted by Kastas, waking the boys up and giving each of them a numbered board then leading them off the ship. They had arrived at their destination overnight, the pirate island of Tortuga, which Luke only knew about after overhearing Kastas talk about it with the other boys. It was a buccaneer haven where pirates from all over the globe would meet, trade and drink together, Kastas had said it was the safest place for a pirate to be, no ruling authority, in fact no rules at all for that matter.

The crew re-chained the 30 boys and tugged them off the boat onto a pier, one of a huge cluster that had hundreds of ships docked by it, some were magnificent with intricate carvings and golden rims, whereas others were old and run-down a few with holes in them. The pier system led to a small gateway and some steps that worked their way up a small incline to a host of buildings. The boys didn't get to see the buildings, however, as the pirates stopped at the archway and arranged the boys in neat rows, making them show their numbers to a growing crowd.

From what Luke could tell, the boys were being sold to slave-owners and other pirate crews for the profit of those that had caught them. The older boys were the first to be bought, their size in comparison to the younger boys appealing to the buyers for what reason Luke could not discern. After about an hour of standing beneath a small parasol in the sweltering heat, an incredibly rich pirate captain appeared and began to discourse with the captain who had kidnapped Luke.

"Ahhh, Captain Krael, it has been a while since you brought a decent sample to these shores, may I look?"

"Of course you can, although the best ones are gone I'm afraid."

He was cut short by the other man who raised a finger demanding silence. Krael seemed nervous, his forehead was sweaty and his previously authoritarian posture cowered in front of the other man, which made Luke smile. *There's always a bigger fish.* The smile however was quickly dispersed as the man looked at him dead in the eyes.

"I don't know, Krael, it would appear to me that there may still be some profitable specimens for me to inspect."

He moved with a powerful grace, every move fluid but full of strength. His eyes wondered over the boys, often being drawn back to Luke. He grabbed one boy's jaw and forced his mouth open, carefully inspecting his teeth and then made his way to Luke. He walked around the boy, eyeing him up like a predator, humming his approval as he opened Luke's mouth.

"T'would appear to me that you have caught a rich boy, Krael, that fire scheme of yours seems to have worked marvellously."

Krael looked genuinely pleased but just as he went to reply, he was interrupted.

"I'll take 15 and 24."

And with that he was gone, casually walking up the stairs.

Luke looked down at his number, checking if he had remembered it correctly and his heart skipped a beat, written in charcoal on the wooden board was the number twenty-four.

Agnes Part 1

Captain Lamorte had just got back from Tortuga, his new fighters dragging along behind him, although there were only two of them which surprised Agnes, she was expecting at least a dozen. *Must've been a bad batch.* The captain, as per usual went straight to his quarters and she followed, grabbing a silver jug of wine on the way, knowing that he would ask her for some as soon as she entered. He looked back and smiled at her, a genuine reaction and then walked into the room, holding the door open for her.

"You'd love it up there, Agnes, why don't you come with me to the party tonight?"

"I don't go, Father, because most of those dirty pirates don't know how to respect a woman, in fact most of them don't even know what one looks like. They'd drool over me and I'm not one for the attention."

He looked hurt.

"Oh, come on, there'll be other girls there for them to play with, besides, you'll be with me the whole time and not one of those pirates would dare cross me. I'm their deity."

He laughed, his dimples and laugh-lines showing as he did so.

"I can't go anyways; I have to look after your new prizes."

"Well, I won't force you. Now, pass me that wine, I'm not nearly drunk enough."

He laughed again, this time for longer, making Agnes smile as well. He took the jug and filled his glass; the silver handle glinting in the sunlight that was beaming through the windows at the back of the room. She took it back and smiled whilst watching him take a huge gulp. He leaned forward and stroked her cheek, then chuckled once more before letting out a small burp right into her ear.

"I think I need a refill."

Agnes turned to leave the room, leaving the jug on a short wooden stool by the door.

"God, you're disgusting. Fill it yourself."

He hadn't stopped laughing since the burp but at her comment he began to roar, practically falling off his chair. Agnes closed the door, smiled and went down to the lower cabins where she met the new recruits her father had scavenged. There were two of them, roughly the same age but incredibly different in appearance. One had golden hair; the other had a deep brown that matched his eyebrows. The blonde one was slightly taller than the other boy and looked in much better shape, despite both of them stinking like animals. They did have one similarity, however, they both had the same fierce determination in their eyes, the same unbreakable will. She saw why her father chose them, they would do well here.

She told them where they would sleep and what they would do to keep the ship afloat, although all they were assigned was to mop the deck. She showed them their hammocks and then told them to go for a wash in the sea because she couldn't bear the smell much longer. She pitied them, however; they must have been through hell and back to find themselves caught up in the slave trade. She finished her introduction and left the cabins for the deck, hoping to watch the fireworks from the crow's nest.

The captain had left for the party with most of his crew, leaving her alone to her thoughts. She liked the boys, they were well mannered and disciplined but she did not wish to know who had trained them and what inhumane methods they had used to achieve such results. *They won't know how lucky they are that the captain found them, they may hate what he turns them into but at least he'll treat them like humans.*

The fireworks were so magnificent that they shook the island. The hounds however thought otherwise and hid with the crew members that had to look after the new fighters. At the top of the mast, she could see everything, people drinking and singing and dancing. Part of her wished she had gone but she was never a social person or at least not social with pirates. Almost on cue two men fell out of a bar door locked in a drunken fist fight as others cheered and made bets on their chosen champion. One of the men was clearly better than the other who moved slow and crookedly, she felt bad for him. The brawl ended with the stronger man pulling out his knife and placing it against the other's throat, surprisingly not going for the kill; instead he kicked him in the head and walked away. Agnes was amazed, the only explanation she could come up with was that they were of the same crew or family because pirates rarely let their opponents live. The man who had been kicked lay unmoving on the floor but from her distance, Agnes couldn't tell if the man was alive or dead. Captain Lamorte opened the inn door and stumbled out of it, not noticing the collapsed man on the floor and his crew followed in drips and drabs, a few with their arms around women. One of the crew knelt down beside the man and shouted something inaudible to the Captain who turned and paced towards the injured pirate. It seemed they were as concerned for the man as Agnes was but the Captain walked away, which left his men to carry the almost lifeless body to the ship along the endless wooden piers.

Agnes watched from the crow's nest as the man was lifted onto the ship, she only knew he was alive by the ragged breaths he was taking. Normally she wouldn't be too concerned for the life of another pirate but this man was old and weathered and she pitied him like an old dog, past his purpose but still going through life. She wondered why a man would want to attack him, he could hardly have been a threat to them. The Captain had left for his cabin but returned carrying bandages and a sling; the man's injuries weren't bad but for an old man they must have been excruciating, although he fought quite ferociously for someone his age. *He's been through worse than that, the old sea dog.* Agnes watched until the man was all cared for, a sling on his arm and some bandages on his head and leg, when she was sure he was okay, she turned her attention back towards the sky.

The black stretched out endlessly, dotted with bright stars and great swirling patterns that were edged with purples and pinks. Her pale blue eyes tracked them and in her mind she made shapes and images. The air was crisp and humid, summery despite it being December, although Tortuga remained the same temperature all year round, a paradise for those who liked the warmth. Agnes didn't mind it herself but she loved the change in seasons, she loved watching the leaves on trees turn from greens to yellows and reds and then seeing the trees empty, like skeletons, and then the leaves would return with the migrating birds just to start the cycle all over again. She admired it. She loosened her grip on the rough wooden railing, letting herself lean back against the wind-shocked mast and there she stood for a while, taking deep breaths of the fresh air while her mind wondered. After a few minutes, she began to descend the mast, using the sail's ropes as hoists to ease herself down to the smooth deck.

She crept down the stairs and slipped into her hammock that was suspended from the ceiling above the barrels of rum and wine, the only hammock in the entire room, her room. She peered over towards the boys' cabin where they were all cramped, the hammocks swaying and hitting each other as the ship moved side to side with the waves. It was worse when they were out to sea but luckily for them they were safely tied to the jetty, she was about to turn away until she noticed one of the new boys lying on the floor, his eyes closed. His blonde hair lay loose about his head and his arms were tucked behind his head as a makeshift cushion. *His hammock must have been taken over by the injured old man; he must think himself a real hero.* She turned her head to face the other direction and closed her eyes, calmly drifting off to sleep.

Luke Part 3

Kastas had been hauled on deck, lifeless, Luke only recognising him because of his clothing and bald head. From what Luke had gathered, he had been in a fight with Captain Krael over their next voyage and the feral man had attacked Kastas, which didn't sit right with Luke. *How can you attack a man that has followed you like a slave over something trivial like that?*

Despite his empathy for the old man, Luke was reluctant to let him use his hammock, mainly because he had been looking forward to sleeping somewhere softer than the hardwood boards of Krael's ship. When the time came, however, Luke didn't complain as he knew that the old man would do the same for him if he were injured, which comforted him; at least he had a friend on board. Another friend he had made on the ship was the other slave boy that the Captain bought with Luke, Hal, who was very much like Luke but from a poorer background. Luke saw him as his first ever poor friend. He was, however, still cautious of the lower-class boy.

The crew was disbanded, and they all headed for the cabin that they slept in. It was irritatingly cramped to the point where Luke could hear Hal's breath from above him as he tried to sleep. Every so often the ship would hit the pier it was docked to, shaking the hammocks and scraping the wood with a dreadful noise. It kept Luke awake, so he just sat on the floor, arms behind his head and closed his eyes, resting as best he could but lacking the dark nothingness of sleep.

Just as he was drifting off, he heard a light tap at the cabin door which instantly pricked his ears up. He turned to face the door and peered through the small round window to see the pirate girl turn her head away. Her dark hair swaying with the movement and cascading down her back, Luke was caught in a trance and could not help but stare, although she was out of sight. She was on his mind all night, even though she had been quite blunt and dry when they had first met where she told Luke and Hal what they would have to do to keep the ship clean. Her beauty was obvious but it wasn't that which had captivated Luke, it was her demeanour. She strode the ship like she owned it, despite being a woman, a pirate one at that. Luke felt ashamed of thinking about her, his mother would have been outraged if he brought home a girl like that.

His mind then followed the thought of his mother and father, wondering if they missed him or if they had sent out a search party. Then he remembered his father's ships slowly burning in the dockyards. Everything he wanted to be taken from him. He vowed at that moment to take revenge on the pirates that had captured him and to return to his home one day, however long it might take. He pondered over a plan for many hours but by day break, he felt sure that he would be able to escape this pirate slavery and put an end to the piracy and plunder of these criminals.

Art Part 3

Art had left his little grove and was walking through the jungle without a clue of where to head. He knew he had to find somewhere to hide and his initial though had been up a tree or down a hole or in a cave but they all seemed too obvious. If what was chasing him was intelligent, he would have to find somewhere they wouldn't look, the problem being that he couldn't find anywhere. He though the best plan would be to head to high ground and survey the area, hopefully finding somewhere that fit the bill, so that was what he had done. He had found the tallest tree and climbed it as high as he could go, just above the tops of the other trees and he had spied a mountain, it's jagged, white cliffs dominating the landscape. He walked as straight a path towards it as he could manage, desperate to keep ahead of the storm that the voice had warned about.

The trees began to thin, so he assumed that he was nearing the mountain but the forest seemed to never end and its humidity had begun to take its toll. He was drenched in sweat that made his ripped clothes stick to his body and the darkness had made his eyes grow tired much quicker, not to mention the fact that he hadn't eaten for days. At least, he'd managed to drink some of the morning dew from the huge, curled leaves of the prehistoric looking trees that inhabited the jungle. Every step Art took he felt more alone, more trapped like the trees were slowly squashing the air out of him. He hadn't noticed until now but his fists were clenched and his jaw was locked. The panic he'd felt previously had gone, replaced by a fierce determination and willpower that Art did not know he possessed. He promised himself he would survive and trudged on, ploughing through the bushes that painfully scratched at his skinny legs. He was going to win this fight and live.

As Art continued down the path, he began to feel a strange energy fill the forest. The hair on his arms and legs began to stand on end and he could hear a buzzing in his ears that reverberated through his body, sending waves of nausea into his stomach. The air around him also changed, it was lighter and colder as if it was being pulled into the sky; the wind picked up and the already dark forest became pitch black. Art stopped walking and instead fell into a full sprint towards what he hoped would be the end of the jungle. He could barely see his feet, so he had to slow his pace slightly so as not to run into a tree or a ditch and eventually he found himself at the edge of the jungle, staring up at the sky that had become a swirling maelstrom of dark clouds.

The fog that surrounded the island was rising high into the sky and joining the clouds to form a giant black funnel. The clouds began to change colour, flashing green before turning to a deep purple that blended with the black and blanketed the whole sky, covering the sun. Lightning crashed down from the heavens and lit the sky in a beautiful iridescent aura of blue and white light; it was accompanied by a low rumble of thunder that shook the ground with its shear ominous power.

Art was taken aback by the calamity that was unfolding above his head; he almost wanted it to take him, its magnificence drawing him in. He was snapped out of his trance by a howl that came from within the forest, its long piercing note adding to the ruckus of the storm. It sent shivers down Art's spine. He stepped backwards, his back pressing against the sharp stone of the mountain, he didn't want to move but managed to drag himself away.

The mountain was littered with crags and holes but they weren't big enough for Art to fit, making him panic more and more until he could barely control his movements. He could not find somewhere to hide. He ran along the length of the cliff keeping his hand pressed against the rock in an attempt to not get lost in the eternal black of the storm. The howling started once more, this time closer but Art still hadn't found an escape in the steadfast rock that could lead to his survival, however, just as he began to lose hope, his hand slipped through the stone which sent him tumbling to the hard ground. The boy jumped back up, a primal energy filling his fatigued muscles that sent him running into the cave to find shelter and protection from the storm and whatever manner of creature it had awakened. His hand was slick with rain or blood, Art could not tell and traced the edge of the cave which was heading down into the bowels of the mountain but he followed it without a second thought, frenzied by the possibility of being caught be the things in the storm. His wet feet slipped and stumbled through the cave, eventually leading to a small opening in the wall that he clambered into, just barely big enough for his scrawny frame to fit, and there here waited.

Art was sure that he would be found and killed but within him hid a small amount of hope that he clasped onto through the storm. He was deathly silent, hardly breathing and listening out for the slightest of noises, however, the ferocious pat of rain mixed with the thunder made it impossible until he heard panting. Right beside his face. His body froze and he stopped breathing altogether, one of the creatures was hunting his scent and had found him. It had stopped inches from his face but in the dark neither he nor the beast could see each other, Art only knew he was there because of the rhythmic pants it let out. Whatever it was, it couldn't have been hunting by smell or Art would have been caught, at least that's what he thought, so he tried his best to be as silent as possible. He was desperate to breathe but too scared to do so. Eventually he began to feel feint, a dull pain throbbing in his stomach from holding it in for so long. He focussed all his energy on holding his breath longer but his mind was stolen away by an itching feeling in his lower back and then his cheek and arms that made him want to jolt up. He brushed off whatever was crawling on his skin; it was hairy and had more legs than Art wanted to imagine but in the act of swiping at the insects he let out a long breath and then sucked in another out of shock. The monster instinctively turned to face Art. He could feel its rancid breath on his cheeks and his stomach knotted in fear but just as Art expected it to strike, a massive boulder collapsed off the cave wall and landed on top of the creature pushing out its last breath with a short wheeze and a gargle.

Art stayed motionless, his body quivering in his hiding spot out of the surge of adrenaline that had pumped into his bloodstream. There were howls still coming from outside the cave that echoed through the empty stone but they sounded different to the howls that had begun the hunt. *I think they're leaving.* Art didn't want to risk leaving his crevice so he waited until he was certain that the beasts were gone at which point he wriggled out onto the cave floor. He stood up and wiped himself off, more insects falling off his wet body; he shivered in response and stamped his feet where he thought they had fallen, hoping to squash them. He stopped killing the bugs and began to realise that he did not know which way was out of the cave, he had no light to guide him and the sounds that he assumed were coming from the outside world were echoing all around him and bouncing of the stone walls so that he could not pinpoint where exactly they were coming from. He once again felt alone and scared with no one to help him like there always had been. His resolve had faded and he lost all hope.

He decided to just pick a path and follow it but the giant boulder had blocked the path. *At least, I know the way out.* Art had no option but to follow the route that led further into the mountain.

Walking cautiously, he made his way through the cave, its surfaces growing smoother and wetter the further down he went. As the rocky wall continued it began to curve, revealing a sparkling green light at the end of the dark tunnel, deep below a steep decline that Art had no way of climbing down. He examined his possibilities if he slid down he would not be able to come back up but he could not stay in the cave or turn back. *What option do I have?* After some thought, he sat down on the wet floor and pushed himself to the edge of the ramp, teetering. Eventually, he made the jump and slid down the damp tunnel, falling into a pool of water that was lit with luminescent crystals of pink and green. The pool was expansive and filled with them but instead of confused or worried, Art was amazed, gazing into the bright colours with a childish sense of bewilderment.

The water was clear and refreshing and glinted with the light from the crystals. Art drank greedily from it and swam towards the edge, wanting to touch the beautiful gems but as he neared them he stopped, suddenly aware of a small pair of eyes that were watching him from the roof of the cave. Art stared back through a dazzling waterfall that flowed out from the smooth wall the creature was clasping onto. It was illuminated by the green light, its black fur a stark comparison to the bright crystals. From what Art could tell, the creature had wings, long and leathery and large green eyes that seemed as frightened as Art's. It let go of the wall and flew to a large crystal that it perched on upside down, keeping its eyes on Art but its bashfulness was replaced with curiosity. It tilted its head but remained motionless. Art slowly made his way towards it, his own fear slightly repressed by the size of the creature in front of him, for it was only about the size of a melon. As Art stepped closer, it flapped its wings and Art acknowledged that it wanted to be left alone but continued to lock eyes with it. The tiny hands on the end of its wings twitched in rhythm with the twitching of its short snout.

"Don't worry, little fella, I don't want to hurt you."

"Well, how do I know that?" it replied.

Art fell back in shock.

"Did you just?"

"Speak?"

Art's eyes widened and his jaw hit the floor, he was completely taken aback. He got up off the ground and stepped backwards, right to the edge of the pool, suddenly wanting to be out of the cave and away from this thing.

"I speak quite often actually, although I'm confused as to why you're shocked. After all, we've already conversed."

Agnes Part 2

At sunrise, after three nights in Tortuga, the ship finally set sail for the Arena and Agnes was ecstatic. She hated the mess of Tortuga and its loud angry customers, so finally getting away was a relief. The water gave her a sense of belonging, it was expansive and when calm, it shimmered under the sun. Normally she would hate being trapped with a bunch of pirates for weeks on end but she loved Lamorte's crew like family and they loved her back, making the voyages they went on full of fun and laughter. What she had noticed by being around other crews in Tortuga was how they didn't have the same bond her crew did, they were acquaintances rather than friends, most of them just hired labour. She was grateful for the company she took.

The wind was with the sails and the ship floated swiftly over the glassy blue, effortlessly dragging them towards the Arena where the new recruits would be broken in and made into killing machines that would garner a huge wealth for the Captain or at least that's what he hoped. There were already countless gladiators in Lamorte's custody but they didn't last long and he liked to have a fresh reserve. These two however were younger than his usual fighters, a good few years from reaching the age deemed worthy of fighting in the pits. From what Agnes could tell, the two boys the Captain had bought were weak and desperate; they'd take a long time and effort to train and time was not a commodity that pirates tend to have. At the top of the mast, however, Agnes had all the time in the world.

Gusts of wind blew her dark hair back, pushing it off her shoulders and into the air like some sort of cape. She was always the watcher in the crow's nest, it had been her job for as long as she could remember and she revelled in every second of it. No one to talk to or please, just open skies, open seas and her own thoughts. Even when she wasn't on duty, she found herself climbing the many ropes and nets that led up the great oak mast that pierced the deck and buried itself deep in the bowels of the ship.

Looking down, she could see the crew busy, some holding and securing ropes, others playing cards and some catching the sun. Even the Captain himself was lounging on a chair just behind the wheel. The only two that didn't look comfortable were the new recruits. She hadn't bothered with names, expecting them to die before she'd ever need to use them. They did try their best though, following her instructions from their initial meeting and for the most part they did well, although the Captain did shout at them a few times, mainly for some motivation. She smiled and turned back to the horizon.

By the time she had climbed down, the sun was setting and the sails had been furled, letting the crew sleep without having to worry about the ship going too far in the wrong direction. She slipped off the last rope, landing graciously onto the deck with a slight thud and made her way to her cabin. The room was dark and cold, the smell of liquor wafting in the air.

"Captain," she said smiling.

"No sneaking up on you is there?"

"What do you want?" she asked.

"Just wanted to see if you're all right. You've been up that mast all day. And you've hardly eaten."

He threw her a chunk of bread with a hunk of ham crudely wedged into it.

"Thank you."

She nibbled the edges like a hesitant mouse, holding eye contact with the Captain through the darkness.

"Well, at least you've got manners…not hungry?"

She didn't say anything.

"If you ask, I'll leave."

"Go then," she remarked bluntly.

The man didn't move.

"What?"

She knew that he was holding in a giggle, which aggravated her even more.

" I changed my mind."

"Turn on a light then and stop acting like a kid," she conceded.

He felt for the lantern that she kept on her nightstand and flicked the switch, lighting the oil inside with a warm flame. She looked up at him, and then looked to the floor, still chewing on the bread.

"Game? Good, I'll get it ready." He didn't wait for her reply. "Oh, come on, sit down, you oaf and join in, I miss you!"

"I saw you this morning, what more do you want?"

"Oh, don't be facetious; you know that's not what I meant. Now start dishing out hands 'cause I'm not doing everything; I am the Captain if you didn't realise."

"I'm not a pirate if you didn't realise," she returned with just as much sarcasm.

"Just because some code says girls can't be pirates doesn't mean that you're not one to me."

She stared back at him through her brow, raising her forehead with a callous look.

"What do you want to play? Ahh, Wit and Reason, good choice." He didn't wait for her reply this time either, which just made her angrier.

I just want to be left alone.

"If looks could kill…I think I should leave before you pull that sword on me."

His eyes drifted to the sabre lying on her wardrobe and then back to her. After a couple of seconds, he left the room, laughing as he went.

"Oh, and before I go, I thought it best to tell you that you're not on watch tomorrow."

"What!" she exclaimed. "But…"

"…I was just joking!" he interrupted, following up his remark by erupting in laughter and promptly shutting the door. He laughed all the way to his own cabin.

Agnes wasn't always so clipped with the captain. There was a time when they would chat for hours and laugh together but as she grew older she came to appreciate her time alone. She hoped he understood that she meant well but he was always so hurt by the rejection and she didn't know how to put it across. He was everything to her but she just needed her space.

The next day was the same as the day prior and the days before that, Agnes watching whilst the crew arduously led the ship towards the Arena. For weeks, the routine remained the same, only changing when extra hands were needed on deck. The only excitement of the voyage being a small ship spotted on the horizon heading south, the crew did debate whether to follow it and board it, possibly capturing the sailors and their bounty but the captain wanted his cargo offloaded before any more was stacked onto his ship, the Oceanus. When Agnes finally spotted land, they had been sailing for around four weeks, slower than expected but that was understandable considering the weight the poor vessel was carrying.

The ship was a flurry of motion, the crew tirelessly holding, securing and then unhitching ropes to guide the ship towards the docks. Initially Agnes was upset to leave the ship but she was fond of Lamorte's private dwellings by the Arena and the fact that he owned the entire complex let her roam it peacefully without having to deal with other pirates, except for those that were part of the crew. Winds pushed them towards a myriad of wooden jetties and the pirates hooked the Oceanus onto the huge wooden posts sunk beneath the waves that kept her steady. Agnes was the last to leave ship, dragging her small collection of belongings onto the weathered jetty. She followed the stone steps towards the captain's house by the beach and set her stuff down just outside her room's door. Lamorte was drinking and gambling in the kitchen with a couple other crew members giggling and gossiping like an over excited schoolboy. *He'll leave that room with less money than he entered it with, that's for sure.* She was pleased that he was happy; it had taken him a long time to even smile let alone laugh and she was relieved that he had finally achieved some semblance peace.

The Arena itself was situated a little ways off the coast, a huge stone coliseum with smaller barracks built beside it, although they were overshadowed by the immense size of the Pits. Agnes didn't bother heading straight there and instead walked towards the open savannah to watch the magnificent African sunset and enjoy the picturesque landscape. After finding a comfortable place to sit, she opened her small casket and began munching on the leftovers from breakfast admiring the beauty that lay sprawled out in front of her.

There were mountains in the distance, rivers flowing from them into the grassy plains that stretched for countless miles in either direction. Where the rivers met there were great lagoons teeming with life and beside those where great expanses of grassland, dotted with small gatherings of trees that gently shifted in with the breeze. The red rays of the sun painted it all with a glorious crimson glow, beaming through the few clouds that cushioned the azure sky. It was stunning.

Art Part 4

"That was you?" Art stuttered.

"I'm assuming you're referring to the voice that warned you about the storm. Yes, that was me."

Art stopped for a moment, awestruck. His eyes were wide in curiosity and confusion, a combination that made him feel dizzy.

"I'm Kela though, thanks for asking."

"But…but you sound so different. You sounded like some monster but now you sound like a woman. How?"

"My magic isn't quite as strong anymore; it stops me from being able to sound like me when I speak long distance. I rarely speak to anyone normally anyways, so it hasn't made much of a difference. I'm glad you're here though, I needed some company."

It smiled as best it could and held eye contact with Art, making him feel slightly uncomfortable.

"So why didn't you tell me to come here in the first place rather than being so vague?"

"You know that would've been smart. Then you'd be safe and I'd have company. Wow, I'm impressed. I'll do that next time."

Art grew visibly angry and turned his attention to finding an exit to this underground grove. There didn't seem to be anywhere that led to the surface, just a few cracks in the cold stone that were either dead ends or heading deeper into the Earth.

"Oh, there won't be a next time. I'm going to find my way out of this cave and then off this island."

"Why would you want that? Thought you didn't like your old life."

"I...wait, how'd you know that?"

"You told me."

"Umm, no I didn't."

"Oops, that's awkward. A good guess then..."

Art wasn't convinced but didn't want to know how anyways, he was dead set on finding a way out.

"You won't find the way out looking there."

Art ignored it. His frustration was growing and he was becoming increasingly aware of the fact that he was trapped. *If it speaks again, I'll rip its wings from its body.*

"Excuse me? It? I'm a she. Also, what's with the anger? I'm only trying to help."

"Please, don't read my mind. I'm not going to ask how you can do it; I just want you to stop."

"Understandable."

"Please...just tell me where the exit is and I'll get out of your hair."

Art looked back at her, giving her a very synthetic smile.

"Fur. Not hair."

"That's beside the point, I need to get out of here and you know how."

"I don't want you to leave, I like company," she sneered back.

"Well, feel free to come along," Art said with his arms wide in gesture.

"Really?"

The bat looked genuinely excited by the proposition.

"No, not really, you've irritated me enough already."

"No backsees, my fingers were crossed."

"You don't even have fingers."

In response, Kela extended her wing and wiggled two tiny finger-like appendages in the air. Art turned away again, his fist clenched. He wasn't just angry, however, he was surprised. Normally he wouldn't talk to anyone, taking after his mother's preference of solitude, so speaking this much to a bat no less was a big shock. The bat just sat and watched as he searched the cavern, slowly turning her head to follow his movements. Hope began to dwindle inside of Art as he exhausted every possible spot for a way out. Eventually, he gave in.

"Please, could you help me? I'll let you come along for a while, just please, tell me the way out."

Kela said nothing, a welcome surprise to Art and tilted her head back towards the cave ceiling. There, hiding between two light green crystals was a hole that led up and out of the cavern.

"How am I supposed to get up there?"

"Watch this."

Art faced the bat and watched her. Nothing happened.

"Watch what?"

"Shhh! I can't do it when you talk to me."

Art put his hands up in apology and once again focussed on the bat. Initially nothing happened but after a few seconds, she began to grow. First her wings stretching wider and wider, then her body and legs expanded and finally her head. The bat had gone from the size of a melon to the size of a large cow. Art was stunned by this show of power.

"Climb on," Kela said smiling.

Art clambered onto her back and held on tight as she leaped of the ground and began to beat her wings, sending the pair rocketing towards the escape.

"Where are we going then?" she asked.

Art had to think for a few seconds before he could answer.

"I don't know." He shrugged.

The bat stopped mid-flight, just as they entered the tunnel and turned her head back to face Art.

"Well, that's helpful!" Kela's sarcasm hit a nerve and Art began to feel guilty.

She restarted her flight and sped through the dark tunnel, air whisking Art's hair off his face. The journey was short and before Art knew it, they were out of the cave and into the night sky. Kela spent little time in the air however and landed almost as soon as they had left the tunnel. Art slid off her furry back and watched as she shrunk back to her original size.

"What do you mean you don't know?"

"I have nowhere to go," Art replied honestly.

"That's surprisingly useful news. If that's the case, then I think we can help each other."

"What do you want then?" Art sighed.

"Well, you've experienced the storm and its…surprises, so you know that it isn't good for the island. I need to get rid of it."

"You can't get rid of a storm; you just have to wait for it to pass."

"Not this storm. This storm comes from a crystal, similar to those you saw in the cavern but it's evil, full of malice. I need you tell help me destroy it."

"You seem powerful enough, why do you need my help?"

"Two heads are better than one and there are some complications. The tribe worship it like a deity; they wouldn't let anyone near, especially not me. If that wasn't bad enough, it's also guarded by those beasts and they're not friendly either. So, in short, I need you to get rid of the tribe and the monsters so I can get to the crystal."

"Have you seen me? I'm not exactly a warrior."

"Well, hopefully you won't have to fight. You raise a fair point though, in a fight against yourself I don't think you'd win. In combat, you would die quite quickly." Kela laughed slightly, her attempt at stifling it failing.

"It's not funny; I don't want to die."

"Well for…insurance purposes we should at least get you a weapon."

Art prayed that he would not fall into any circumstance that required the use of a weapon but he agreed that it was a good idea to make sure he was as safe as possible. It actually made him feel a bit better, a comfort in the fact that he wouldn't be entirely helpless even though he had no idea how to use a weapon. For the rest of the night, the two got some rest beneath the stars, both anxious to make a safe plan to somehow get to the crystal unseen.

Thankfully for Art, the sun took its time and let him get some sleep, however, disturbed it was. After waking up, the rest of the morning was spent scavenging for food, which satiated Art's hunger and renewed some of his energy. Both of them were silent throughout the meal, although it was uncomfortable for Kela who would rarely stop talking. The situations that did hold her tongue were when she was eating or focussing on something. Eventually Art broke the silence and they conversed the rest of the morning away devising a plan to get Art a weapon from the tribe without being spotted. A few ideas were put forward but they all had some flaw or another that could cost them, however, they did eventually find a plan that seemed to work well and use their few strengths well.

"So, just so we're on the same page," said Art. "The plan is for you to shrink your size and disturb the tribe when they are sleeping and then cue me to lure them towards the beach. With the camp empty of hunters and poorly guarded, you'll be able to grab a weapon, change size again and fly out unnoticed."

"It'll have to be a big distraction to get as many of them out as possible but they're very superstitious and fear the night, so the likelihood is that they'll take as large a force as possible to see what's up."

"This better work," he mumbled.

"For both our sakes," she replied.

Simultaneously they rubbed their necks and scratched at their chins, then without uttering a word they walked towards the hunters' camp.

Luke Part 4

Luke was once again trapped on a ship full of bandits, this time a slave rather than just a prisoner. This journey however was shorter; taking him from the pirate island of Tortuga to somewhere he guessed was at the lower tip of Africa. The landscape was a scorched wasteland where the only plants were thick yellow grasses that poked at Luke's hand as he tried to run his fingers through them. The ground was also lifeless, just dirt and sand, that itched on Luke's skin and lodged itself in his eyes. He was dragged from area to area on the massive compound that the pirates called the Arena, which was to be his home whilst he was enslaved under the Captain. They said that here he would learn to fight as a gladiator until he was old enough to compete in the Pits, where Luke assumed he would be put against slaughtering machines and forced to kill them for the sport and entertainment of pirate audiences. The whole idea made Luke feel nauseous; he was an academic not a fighter.

The day was waning and Luke was still to be shown where he would sleep for the night but he knew that the pirates would want him well rested if he was going to train and fight for the benefit of their treasury. The pirate showing them around was a short red-headed man with fewer teeth than feet but it was his temper that was his defining feature. His fuse was short and Luke was tempted to light it but this man seemed reckless and aloof, a dangerous partnership when paired with a mean temper. *I suppose I can't expect a pirate to act with restraint, the uneducated weasel.* Luke stared him down throughout the tour, silently judging him and it seemed the man knew because whenever he looked at Luke his voice would deepen very slightly and his speech would grow louder.

Eventually, the man showed the two boys their living quarters which was just a small dingy cage with two straw mattresses in the centre and a hole dug in the ground that led to what Luke guessed to be some underground sewage system. But just as the boys began to walk into their new home, the man grabbed Hal's shoulder and hauled him to a separate room down the hall. Luke didn't know where Hal was taken but he could hear the screams from his cell and a sharp anxiety began to seep into him. The two were gone for a while before Luke saw them again but Hal was changed. His dark brown hair was matted with blood, mud and tears and his face was a mess of scratches and bruises. By far, the most grisly thing about him was his back. Blood seeped through his ripped caramel shirt and dripped down his legs leaving a crimson trail behind him and a pool of blood where he stood. The bone of his spine was bare and his skin had been lacerated by what looked like a thousand wounds. He was crying but remained unmoving and looked at Luke with a terror in his eyes, any hope the boy had was beaten out of him. Luke's hope also faded and was replaced by anger for this poor excuse of a man before him. *How? How could you mortally beat an already impoverished boy to the ground?* Luke also began to cry at the sight of his friend. The man left Hal to his suffering and made for Luke, an evil snigger in his eye as he yanked the terrified boy away from the bars of the cage. Luke went cold. The man's vice-like grip led Luke to the same room it had taken Hal but Luke did not look up. Instead he stared at the trail of blood, still slick on the floor and vomited.

When Luke was shoved into the room, he was expecting to be alone with the ginger man but sat eagerly in the corner was the Captain, whip in hand.

"Turn around boy."

He had lost the sense of humour he appeared to have at Tortuga and it was replaced by a spiteful grimace. The man seemed to both enjoy and despise the torture simultaneously.

Luke did what he was told and turned to face the wall that still glistened with the evidence of Hal's encounter. His shirt was ripped by the ginger man and the Captain went straight to hitting Luke with the full force of his blows. Great gouts of blood gushed out of the gouges that the whip carved into Luke's back. The lashing pain grew more intense every hit until Luke was screaming in agony, begging the Captain to stop but the man continued thrashing him to the rhythm of his breath. He did not hold back and when he'd had his fun with the whip, he told the red-head to finish the job and he did so with his own two hands. The Captain was content and left the room and Luke's agonising screams behind.

Luke returned to the cage battered and bruised, his own blood mixing with Hal's trail on the floor, painting a gruesome scene. Both boys spent the evening crying, neither talking to each but both feeling each other's pain. A slight breeze drifted through the empty halls and soothed Luke's back slightly but not enough to ease the unendurable agony cause by the myriad of slashes and bruises that coated his body. The night was slow and sleepless and by the time morning came neither boy could move or speak; they were immobilised by the pain.

With the rise of the sun, came the ginger pirate who brought with him two plates of what looked like food but smelt awful, the stench making Luke retch. His stomach, however, ignored the warning that his nose gave him and Luke inhaled the food, the taste only partially less potent than the smell. Hal also ate the food, although much more hesitantly. *Surely he's used to eating rubbish like this, isn't that what the poor eat normally?* The ginger pirate left them no time to digest and pulled them out of the cage and towards the pits that had been organised specially for training. Both boys were exhausted and terrified but the ginger pirate didn't care. To him they were just livestock, his loyal subjects.

"I'm Aaron and I'm going to train you for the next few weeks to see if you're up to much. If you're not, I'll be personally skewering you with this here sword." He gestured to the cutlass hanging by his side, crudely tied to a belt with rope. "That means that if you don't do as I say then you'll be beaten, if you talk without being spoken to, you'll be beaten and if you can't complete a task I set, you guessed it, you'll be beaten."

Aaron was enjoying their pain too much. The boys were listening intently, despite their wounds nagging at them and making them cringe with any small movement. One of Hal's wounds had opened up and as Luke turned to him, the boy vomited onto the ground where a pool of his blood was beginning to spread.

"I'd eat that back up if I were you; that meal this morning might just be the last you eat for a while."

Hal made no movement, he just hung his head in shame.

"No no no. That's not how this is going to work. I said eat it."

Aaron rested a hand on his cutlass. Hal looked from the floor to the pirate and back again, then slowly drooped to all fours and began to eat the muck. The sick had mingled with the blood and had turned orange, which made Luke gag.

"Ooops. Careful there, if you're sick as well, you'll be doing the same thing."

Luke grimaced at the man when he wasn't looking, his anger boiling into rage. The hatred fuelled his body and he forgot all sense of pain for a split second before a gargling sound from his left pulled him back to reality. Hal had begun gagging and had stopped eating. Aaron languidly moved up to him like a predator and placed his boot on Hal's head, squishing his face into the mess of blood and puke.

"What have we here? You can't complete a task that I set. If I recall correctly, that means punishment. Doesn't it? Well? Doesn't it?"

"Yes, Aaron," Hal timidly replied, his lips jittering in fear.

"No," Luke said, looking at the ginger pirate through his eyebrows.

He didn't know where it came from but he regretted it almost instantly. Aaron looked up, straight into Luke's eyes, his nostrils flaring with a fire burning in his eyes.

"Oh, you're gonna regret that, you little shit!"

Luke watched as the man pounced at him and drew his cutlass. He closed his eyes as the blade came whistling through the air, hurtling towards his head. They remained closed for what felt like an eternity but the impact never came. Instead, what Luke heard was a wet thud and a crack. He opened his eyes as Hal's body fell at his feet. At first, he didn't realise what had happened but it soon dawned on him as he watched the pool of ruby ichor expand. Luke looked down to see Hal squirming in pain, an arm detached and laying limp beside him.

Luke fell to his knees and held the body of his friend. He remained still as the captain came rushing in and grabbed the boy calling for some medical help. He ripped a part of his shirt and tied it just above the wound to staunch the flow of blood. Hal was carried away from the pits by the Captain and handed to another pirate. Lamorte returned without Hal but with his cutlass in hand. He strode towards Aaron and Luke, who both flinched as the enraged pirate lifted his blade. Once again, Luke heard a wet crunch but didn't feel anything. Luke turned in horror to see Aaron's face cleaved in two, immortalising his petrified expression. All sorts of liquids oozed out of the red-head's nose and eyes as his lifeless body collapsed onto the ground, his corpse awry and twitching. The Captain said nothing and returned to where he had come from, leaving Luke alone in the dusty coliseum, crying and shaking from the trauma.

Agnes Part 3

Agnes had been told to look after the blonde boy whilst his friend was recovering. She was taking a morning walk when she saw him being carried to the medical building attached to the Arena, its size smaller than most of the other buildings because most fighters died before they could be healed, so it was rarely used. The dark-haired boy's injuries were devastating; his arm had been cut right through and his back was stacked with slash marks from a whip. *Whoever beat him made a good job of putting the poor boy in as much pain as possible. They had to have been a monster to let him suffer so much.* Her initial instinct was to run to the boy and help him but it was not her place, he was the Captain's plaything, not hers. All Agnes could do was hope that he recovered as the Captain would be dangerously angry if he died, after all, he did spend money on the boy. After she was assured the boy would live, Agnes was instructed to check up on the other fighter who had not left the Pits since the gruesome scene. Shaking all over, he looked a mess, great streaks on his face where his tears had wiped away at the grime. Agnes felt bad but from what she had heard, the other boy's injuries were caused because of this boy being unable to keep his mouth shut, although he was the only person alive who could recall the story. The Captain had made sure of that.

Agnes led him back to the cages and brought him some food and water; he thanked her and took it but did not look her in the eyes. He seemed ashamed of himself and labelled himself as guilty for the attack but Agnes knew that it would have been Aaron that was the main perpetrator. *That weasel, he's ruined one boy's life, scarred another and gotten himself killed, not the best pirate there ever was.*

The air was cool that day, a gift from a higher power to ease the heat of the sun. Agnes spoke with Luke about what had happened but he kept some details to himself, including who had whipped him the night before as though he were ashamed of it and wished to bear the burden alone. For hours, the two sat conversing but Agnes still hadn't learned the boy's name, she didn't bother asking, she just listened to him, knowing that he needed to let his thoughts out more than dealing with small talk. He often repeated the same phrases, his words stuttering as he tried to verbalise his stress from the event. When he had finished, they were sat only inches apart, with Agnes leaning in to show her interest in what he was saying, to her it was just courteous but to him it seemed like it meant the world. *He's only a few years younger than me and yet he's been through so much.* He never spoke a word of his past, except that he missed his parents, which touched Agnes as she couldn't remember her mother.

When midday came, Agnes left the traumatised boy and headed to the Captain's shack where the man was drinking a cold beverage beneath the sun. His hands had been cleaned but his clothes were still stained red and his eyes were tired, sinking slightly from the bright rays. He seemed to care deeply for the boys like he did most of his fighters but he was always fond of those helpless and young, that's why he was so attached to Agnes because to him she was alone and afraid. They were a perfect pair despite their bickering and irritating each other at times and she loved him and he loved her. They were an odd family but the only true one Agnes had ever had. She sat and listened to him as well, hardly uttering a word herself, she just nodded and smiled along with him.

When the time came, Agnes left Lamorte's company and headed for her own room to take a nap and eat but she didn't make it far before he called after her to wait for him. He told her to look after the blonde boy, care for him and make sure he trained, ate and slept well. He had a feeling that this boy was going to be a great asset to his roster of fighters. Agnes herself had sensed his willpower when chatting with him. He was never going to give up or let others boss him around for long; Aaron was a clear example of this. Fire burned within him, an educated sense of pride that burst through his eyes even if he meant to hide it.

On the way there, Agnes bumped into the old man Kastas who was almost fully healed, his arm minutely twisted from the break but nothing too noticeable. It seemed as though he was going to check out the Arena and probably see what all the commotion was. He had also been assigned to ensure the well-being of the boys but as their trainer, a much more docile one than the fiery short-tempered red-head they had before. Agnes suspected that Kastas would be a much better trainer, especially after his heroic stand against his former captain, Krael, where he showed his combat prowess despite his older age.

When Agnes finally reached her cabin, she sank into her bed and slept the day away, awaking to shouts from the other room where the Captain and the crew were playing dice. From what she could tell, the whole crew had been cramped into the room, all of them drinking and singing and dancing. She was tempted to join but first she went to the injured boy upstairs to see if he needed anything. However, when she got there he was asleep, breathing raggedly and his body shook every-so-often, his wounds slowly leaking fluid into his fresh bandages. Wound tightly with a cast, the boys arm was pressed tightly against his body; it had been cauterised and the smell of seared flesh still faintly lingered in the air. Agnes softly closed the door and made for the Arena to check up on the other boy.

She felt as though she had walked this path a hundred times today but she was keen to make sure he was okay. And he was also sleeping but on the cold floor with naught but an itchy straw mattress. Agnes watched him for a while, lost in her own thoughts and eventually sat down on a chair near to the cage. She had no intention of sleeping; she just stood guard whilst watching him without anyone to bother her. Time flew by and before she knew it, the sun had fully set and had encapsulated them in twilight. The air was chill but with only a faint wind, the sounds of the resident animals drifting with it through the Arena. The cold stone walls reflected the silver moonlight, making them seem blue and soft. To Agnes this was home, her second home after the Oceanus and the waves.

After a short time, Agnes moved to the Pits and after checking her surroundings for unwelcome eyes, she picked up a staff from the dirt floor. Aaron's body had only been moved to the edge of the Pits and the stains of the day's bloodshed was still clearly visible but she ignored them and began training with the weapon. Its hard wood had been smoothed by years of use from the gladiators, so it felt good in her hand as she fell into graceful, languid movements like a dance, the staff becoming an extension of her body. It spun and twisted in her grip masterfully, the balance of it making it look effortless to wield, however, it did strain Agnes's muscles as she began hitting the air with it and moving away from the dance-like movements into much more aggressive ones but she kept the fluidity and rhythm of before. It felt good for Agnes to let out some steam under the iridescence of the moon.

For years, she had been secretly coming to the pits at night to train but she never wanted to be a gladiator, she just enjoyed the peace of mind it brought her to hold a weapon in her hand and use it to attack imaginary foes. Her breaths quickened and her heart pounded as she swung the deadly stick through the air, the ends of it creating whizzing sounds that buzzed past her ears and into the dead of night. Her muscles were stretching and contracting with growing fatigue, which caused her movements to slowly lose their ferocity and become wild swings around her. The ache of her fingertips forced her to clench on the staff harder but that only hurt her more and she dropped the weapon, its landing sending echoes through the stands. Agnes gasped in shock, hoping that nobody had heard and frantically eyed the area, desperate not to be caught. Agnes knew that putting herself at risk like that could have dire consequences, so she decided to take a break. She wiped her brow, took a gulp of water and walked back to the boy, following the dark trail of blood to his cage.

When she got there, however, she was surprised to see another pirate watching over the young boy. It was the old man Kastas. His arm was still slung but he no longer limped as he moved, a sign of his injuries returning to normal. The scars and folds of his face were amplified under the moon, giving him a ghostly look that at first frightened Agnes until she realised it was him.

"Kastas," she whispered. "What are you doing here?"

"I'm just checking on him." He pointed at the boy. "I felt bad him being alone, especially after the day he's just had but it seems he's in good company."

Agnes smiled at the compliment and walked up to the man.

"I'll be training him from now on but I could do with some help, I'm only an old man after all."

"Of course but what could I do? Girls aren't allowed to fight."

"Doesn't seem to stop you though, does it?" He smiled.

She went bright red and stared into his eyes in shock.

"Oh, don't worry, I won't tell anyone. They wouldn't believe this old fool anyways."

"Thank you," she mouthed, careful to keep quiet so as not to wake the boy.

"He'll need good food and water after what I'll put him through and that's where you come in or at least that's what the others will think. I'd be grateful if you gave him night sessions much like the ones you have on your own. That way both of you'll improve."

The old man smiled at her, the wrinkles on his face folding as he did so.

"I'd best be off and I recommend you sleep as well Agnes."

With that he stepped away from the chair and made his way out of the barracks, leaving Agnes once again alone with the boy and her thoughts.

Luke Part 5

Luke ran his sweaty hands through his wavy blonde hair. The sun was beating down on his back as he swung his cutlass through the air. Kastas was intently watching him, hitting his arm with a hardwood stick if he made the wrong move or lost balance, the same he had been doing for the last eight years. Agnes was watching from the side lines as well, although she was less interested, just out in the Pits to get away from the Captain and pretend to do something important. Luke's muscles rippled in the amber rays with every stroke, the air effervescing at the edge of the blade as the young man traced arcs in the sky.

The cutlass wasn't Luke's preferred weapon but he had to make do with what he had in the Pits, so Kastas insisted that he train with each weapon with as much effort as possible so as to have the upper hand on his opponents. Kastas, along with Agnes, had trained Luke to become a fighting machine, so he wasn't as worried about losing as not putting a good enough show on for the audience.

It was around noon when Kastas asked for a break and Luke did not argue. He was exhausted. Agnes's training the night before had bruised him all over, although he did manage to gain the upper hand on the woman who had also become remarkably skilled in combat and even more so in tactics. Over the years the two had formed a powerful bond through sweat and blood, training, working and practically living together; they were a pair. The crew would make jokes about it when they returned from their voyages, saying that they were secret lovers but Luke knew Agnes didn't feel that way. To her he was her best friend and nothing more and he had vowed to himself to escape this life he had been stolen into. That vow, however, had slowly faded and now it was just a dream, far from fruition. For the moment at least, Luke had to worry about winning the next fight, although he knew it would be easy. For three months, he had been fighting and he hadn't lost once. The only person that stood a chance against him was Kane, Luke's partner in the Pits. He was slightly shorter than Luke but still tall in comparison to the pirates that paid heaps of gold to watch the two fight together. They were called the Taijitu, a name that had stuck after a Chinese pirate crew had bet on the pair and won a small fortune, chanting the name as they celebrated the victory.

Luke enjoyed the life on some level, he had no responsibilities except those to win the fights but killing others was never pleasant, despite the fact that he had been training for that exact thing for years. At first, Luke though he would get used to it but every kill had eaten away at his conscience and it scared him how numb he had become because of it. His nature was learning, not killing and yet he had learned such a mastery of killing that he had lost his keenness for academia. He had switched from the pen to the sword to the delight of the Captain that owned a special place in Luke's heart as the man he wanted to kill the most.

The evil man fuelled Luke with a hatred that empowered his strikes because every foe that Luke faced he imagined it was Lamorte and he killed every last one of them. The beatings and whippings he gave hardened both Luke's skin and body and Lamorte loved his creation with a malicious passion. Luke was his greatest asset in terms of gold but also his plaything to let off steam. Luke would be beaten over and over again and no one could do anything about it, hardly anyone cared and amongst those was Agnes but she didn't believe Luke when he told her. He had given up trying to convince her long ago. At least, the other fighters were subdued to the same horrific treatment. It wasn't as though Luke wanted them to be beaten but it gave him comfort that he wasn't the only one.

Hal brought Luke a cup of water and Luke thanked him. The lad was no longer one of the Captain's gladiators, so the man had him become a servant, his personal one. He wasn't beaten like the others were but he still feared the Captain. Behind closed doors, Lamorte could do whatever he wanted to him and Luke didn't want to imagine what dastardly things the pirate lord came up with.

Luke returned the cup and went to go and talk with Kane who was panting heavily and sweating profusely.

"Still unfit then I see."

"Haha. No more than you, rich boy!"

Kane was one of the only people who knew of Luke's heritage and past, the others being his closest friends Hal, Agnes and Kastas but he was the only one of them that liked to bring it up regularly.

"Careful or you'll find your mouth full of dirt."

"You're too slow for me and we both know it!"

"Well, it's good to know that your brain hasn't been damaged from all the wallops you've taken today in training. You must be getting worse with all the times Kastas has knocked you on your backside today. Either that or you're just shit at fighting and need to be beaten like a dog to do something of actual skill."

"I'm sensing some racial undertones there."

The pair laughed and sat on a bench protruding from the hard stone wall.

"We both know that I don't need to resort to race to win an argument with you. All I have to do is hit you hard in the arm, then you'll go crying to your mummy and I'll enjoy the victory,"

They continued laughing as Kastas came over and sat with them. He was an old guy but he hadn't aged a day since Luke had met him. *He's so old that aging itself can't keep up with him.* Luke admired the man though, he was unbelievably strong and hardy, not to mention the only man that had shown him kindness even when he had no incentive to do so. Luke saw him as a father and loved him like one, even when he scolded him for being too lazy or brash. If it weren't for Kastas, Luke was sure that he would have gone crazy or been killed by now but the old man lit the fire of hope within him.

"If you're going to talk, talk tactics would you. Your next fight is in a few days and from what I've heard they aren't hosting any singles events, so you two will have to fight together all day."

"Sounds easy enough," replied Kane, hitting Luke on the arm and winking at Kastas.

"Don't jinx yourselves, I've been told that the greatest fighters from all around the globe are going to be fighting here over the next couple of weeks, so no letting your guard down."

"Of course the best fighters are going to be fighting! I mean we do live here."

Luke chuckled at his friend's answer who also laughed. Kastas was not best pleased.

"Well, if you die out there, I'm having none of the blame. You know for slaves you two are quite bold."

Both of the boys fell quiet before staring down Kastas who eventually conceded.

"Fine. You aren't slaves, you're combat labourers."

The three laughed at the comment, all of them enjoying the humorous moment. It was Kastas who ended the conversation by getting up and walking into the Pits whilst gesturing for the boys to follow.

"Now. I'm aware that you two have become skilled fighters and for that I am both pleased and proud but you lack a certain severity that often saves a man in a combat situation. You have too big hearts and it'll be your empathy that stops you from winning and surviving the fights to come. I want you to look each other dead in the eyes and picture your worst enemy, the person you hate the most other than me. Good. Now pick up a weapon and fight each other."

The pair broke eye contact, the shock evident on their faces.

"When did I say you could break eye contact? I want you two to attack each other with no holding back."

Luke didn't know what to do; he just stared at Kane with a blank expression masking his face. *A few years ago and I would have fought him just for being black but I don't want to hurt him. I've grown up since then. My mind is no longer narrow and selfish.* Kane also seemed hesitant but he made a move to grab a weapon, showing to Luke that he trusted him and Kastas. Luke copied him and grabbed a staff from the weapons rack, the only choice that Luke thought wouldn't hurt his friend but also his preferred weapon. Kane however picked up a cutlass and a dagger, blunted but still deadly. *He really wants to have a go, doesn't he? All right then, let's play.* Luke gripped the staff harder and fell into a battle stance with one end of the staff facing Kane, the defensive position that he often used against Agnes to put her off balance, a combat to her speed. Kane also stooped into a battle stance with his cutlass in front of him and his dagger, in reverse grip, behind him.

"You two are well matched together; your fighting styles are complementary but as adversaries, the table is turned. One of you has the advantage but I want to see if you can figure out who. I'll sit back and watch if you don't mind, my back is playing up but you two feel free to begin."

The pair was locked in an unmoving battle of who would make the first move and begin the fight. Luke surveyed his surroundings to find some sort of advantage but a crowd of other fighters and trainers had encircled the two in a ring. It was exactly like a real pit fight but against Luke's best friend. *It's best if I make the first move, show him who's the boss.* Luke predatorily approached Kane, hoping to catch him off guard with some nonchalance but the other man remained as still as a statue.

"You're quite brave making the first move, Luke, we both know I have the advantage. It's best you sit back like the old man and let me beat you nice an' easy."

Luke smiled back, baring his teeth as he did so, like some sort of snarl, which made Kane sneer in response.

"I don't think you understand what I'm saying. Let me give you a demonstration."

Kane leaped at Luke, both cutlass and dagger reeled in to slash him across the belly, which would have surprised Luke had Kane not said anything. As things were, however, Luke was able to dodge the lunge by slipping past Kane's right side and hitting him on the back with the hardwood staff. Kane just laughed. He lunged again, this time with only his cutlass, leaving his dagger back to block any counters that Luke made. This time, instead of dodging, Luke blocked using his staff with two hands and pushing the cutlass away from his body. However, Kane pre-empted the move and slipped his dagger beneath the staff and cut Luke's shoulder, barely a graze but enough to cause a small stream of blood to trickle down Luke's arm.

"So the giant does bleed. Let's see if he can do some more, shall we?"

"I think I've had my fun, time to play properly," Luke jeered.

They locked eyes and spun around each other, once again stuck in a deadlock of who would attack first but before Luke had a chance to, Kane had already jumped into his guard, dagger pointed straight at Luke's gut and travelling fast. What he didn't know however was that Luke had transferred his weight to his back foot and repositioned himself so that he could trip Kane up using his front foot, which he did just in the nick of time as his friend's blade was millimetres away from penetrating his tanned skin. As Kane was falling, Luke gave him a tap on the back, not enough to cause significant

80

damage but enough to make the young man yelp in pain and surprise. Luke laughed at the sound his friend made, losing focus on the fight and was tripped up himself. The two ended up grappling each other on the dusty floor, throwing punches that missed more often than they connected but by the end they were both bleeding and smiling like feral beasts.

From what Luke could tell they were evenly matched, he couldn't find an entrance to hit Kane and Kane wasn't quite strong enough to break Luke's guard, however, they were both tiring out and sweating copiously. Eventually, Luke realised that neither was going to win with conventional tactics so he switched to a dirtier fighting style, throwing sand and distracting Kane so that he could land consecutive blows. However, Kane caught on quickly and also adapted his fighting style to deal with his hulking friend that seemed impervious to attack; he used his speed to get under his guard and would attack from there, punching the brute a few times before jumping away again to avoid Luke's incoming counter-attacks. Both of them were careful not to use their weapons too much so as not to hurt each other but when it came to fisticuffs neither held back. After trading a few blows, the two stood facing each other, holding their weapon towards the other's neck.

A draw? Yeah, that seems fair.

Gasps echoed from around the crowd and Luke suddenly became aware of the shock on everyone's faces. It seemed as though they wanted to know the stronger member of the Taijitu as much as the pair themselves did. Even Agnes had stopped what she was doing and watched in awe of the two fighters. Luke's and Kane's chests rose and fell rapidly, showing the crowd that the fight was hard for both of them.

"That's the best training session I've had in a while, I've been wanting to beat you to a pulp for quite some time now and judging by your face I did a good job," jeered Kane.

"You should look in the mirror then, your rear end is looking better than your face at the moment. If anyone's the pulp, it's you."

For a second, they stared at each other with snarling grimaces and tension rose between the two young men. What the crowd didn't know was that it was synthetic and the two were playing off the intensity coming from the herd of people. The tension quickly dissipated into laughter and the two men slumped to the ground in exhaustion. Kastas strode over to them looking rather pleased but decided not to speak and instead just watched them as they re-hydrated. The crowd began to disperse, the gladiators being dragged back to training by their masters and after waiting for the last people to leave, Agnes began to talk with the fatigued fighters.

"That was quite the show."

"Ah, just a normal working day for us two hunks," replied Kane in his usual arrogant way.

"Oh, quit acting so confident. Don't forget I kinda own you two."

"Correction," said Luke. "Your beloved Captain Lamorte owns us. In fact, he owns you as well."

Agnes was about to argue back until Kastas stepped in.

"Oh, stop it, you lot, don't ruin the moment with pointless bickering. We're all owned by Lamorte in one way or another, be it through debt, contract or emotion. Now, I'll admit that you two fought well but…"

"Leave out the but for once, please? I'm too tired to hear an old man groan at me!"

"Let me finish, Kane. The but wasn't actually going to be negative; I was just saying that you both need to be careful not to get too cocky. There's a lot of gold on the next few fights and Lamorte has asked me to ensure victory or he'll have all of our heads. Except yours of course, my dear." He nodded to Agnes.

"Well, if I'm not getting in trouble, then I might sabotage these morons and get them killed. It would certainly make my life easier."

Kastas rolled his eyes at her comment and the two young men on the floor just looked at each other and giggled.

"We're worth too much to him for him to just kill us, however, much he wants to. It would be a bad investment," Luke jeered.

"When did you get so smart?" Kane sniggered.

"I'm not smart, it's just common sense."

Luke lied even though he had no reason to, if anything it was so that he wouldn't be linked to that small boy who had a plan for everything and thought the whole world was his. *How wrong I was to think that my life could be written down on a piece of paper and that I would follow that exact plan forever.* Luke smiled to himself, proud of how far he grown.

"I would say get some rest but the Captain's watching, so just pretend like you're doing something while I sit and pretend to watch." Kastas winked.

"Well, you heard the man, Luke, get up and train you lousy swine! Come on porky, up you get."

"Watch your tongue or you'll be having some trouble."

The pair continued training together until night fell and they went back to their cages, except Luke stayed behind in the pits, waiting for Agnes to appear.

Agnes Part 4

Luke was standing in the middle of the Arena, the fading sunlight glinting off his sweat and outlining his brutish physique. He had grown into a tall, handsome and strong young man and Agnes couldn't help but be taken aback by the progress he had made. When she first got to know him, he was an obnoxious little brat that thought he was better than everyone else but over the years through sweat, blood and tears he had evolved into a great friend who takes good care of those he is close to. It was moments like this, when they were alone that she really appreciated his company and she loved him for the man he had become.

As soon as he saw her he smiled and Agnes's heart melted away. He was so innocent and kind but held himself with such authority. Moonlight began to flow over the stands as the last amber rays licked the darkening sky, cascading over the stone and onto the ground like liquid silver. Agnes watched Luke as she approached, watched his breaths rise and fall and watched his eyes avoid her gaze. She moved as close to him as possible to the point where she could feel his warm breath on the top of her head from where he was looking down on her and prodded him in the gut.

"You've got fat."

She looked up to see his hurt expression; however, it quickly dispersed as he tried to play the insult off.

"From the scraps that you give me, I doubt that I'd get fat."

This time Agnes was hurt, although she tried not to show it and instead changed the topic.

"You here to train or make me feel bad?"

"Train, if that's okay with you?"

Agnes decided not to answer with words and pushed Luke over as a response. His reply to that was to tackle her to the ground and pin her to the floor, which didn't end well, as she kneed him straight in the balls. He fell off her, writhing in agony and grasping his groin to try and suppress the pain, which Agnes used to her advantage, kicking him in the back and placing her foot on the collapsed man's leg.

"All right, you win," he said between ragged breaths.

Agnes did feel bad but the victory was still worth it.

"Well, that concludes training. Follow me, I want to show you something."

She grabbed his huge hand and heaved him off the ground, pulling him out of the Arena and into the wilds without checking whether anyone might see them. She was too pre-occupied with containing her excitement at the thought of being able to spend the night with Luke alone and not train. Her heart was racing faster and her stomach was full of butterflies. She was in love with Luke and was finally going to tell him.

The moon lit the grassy planes in its cool white glow and the water reflected it, scattering the radiance over the animals that were grazing and drinking by the river. The air was sweet like nectar and a slight breeze was blowing on the pair's backs, the world was still and timid, even the crickets chirped quieter than usual, encapsulating the moment like a painting. A couple cranes soared above their heads through the cloudless sky and the stars twinkled from the heavens, their light reflecting in Luke's eyes as he looked up to admire them. Agnes had her eyes on Luke's, too captivated to admire the picturesque landscape but when he went to look at her she darted her head away. She felt a fool for avoiding his gaze but the marvel of the moment stole her away once again.

They sat on a rock a few hundred metres away from the Arena and remained silent for quite some time until Luke's curiosity got the better of him.

"Why did you bring me here?"

"No reason, just thought it'd be nice."

Agnes cringed.

"Nice? It's stunning out here. I often forget how beautiful this place is, beyond the gore of the Arena. Then again, I rarely leave the Pits so I suppose it's understandable."

Agnes watched him speak, holding his eye contact before glancing at his lips. She was desperate to say something but didn't know how to word it.

"I love it at night, it's so tranquil."

Come on, Agnes, get to the point!

"It is amazing, I'll admit."

She wriggled slightly closer to him.

"That was a good fight today but why were you two fighting in the first place?"

"Oh, Kastas asked us to."

"You both seemed to enjoy it as well, I thought you two were best friends?"

"We are, but he's a great punching bag."

Agnes laughed, touching Luke's arm as she did so and then turning to face him.

"I could say the same about you."

"You could. If could land a punch on me."

She tried to hit him in response but he caught her arm and pulled her in closer.

"Told you," he whispered. "You're not fast enough."

He moved his gaze back to the river. She continued watching him for a few moments but eventually also looked towards the river, not before wrapping her arm around his and leaning her head on his shoulder. She could hear his heartbeat quicken and saw that his cheeks had turned red. His muscles had gone rigid in shock and Agnes didn't blame him, this was the most intimate they had ever been except the day Hal had lost his arm, it was also a surprise to her but a welcome surprise.

"Relax, Luke; I'm not going to bite."

"Tell that to my balls."

They giggled and she held him tighter, not wanting this night to end. Inside she was desperate to tell him but the fear of rejection was too big a risk. Instead, she stayed quiet and enjoyed the embrace.

Luke Part 6

Luke was frozen. Agnes had wrapped her arm in his and was leaning her head on his shoulder. He felt like he was dreaming. The world around him slowed and he stared into her eyes. He was living the moment that he had wished would come about for years and he didn't want it to end. She was holding him tight enough that he could feel the skin of her arm on his and feel her pulse slowly beat against him. Her hair was cascading down his back, tickling him as the wind gently swayed it to and fro and her hand began to lock with his.

"I can't wait till my fight," he suddenly blurted out, uncomfortable with the silence.

Ahh! You idiot. Now she's going to think all you care about is fighting. His muscles stiffened up again waiting for her reply that he knew was going to be bad.

"I heard it'll be a hard one, you sure you can handle it?"

Luke was relieved that she didn't take the comment the wrong way but he was still uncomfortable and sweating, making his palm slick. He let go of her hand and wiped the sweat off on his torn trousers but didn't pick up her hand again when he was done, he just planted it onto the ground behind it. This move changed his weight and his body moved back, which made Agnes lift her head off of him, her dark hair stroking his arm as she also changed position.

You moron! Now she thinks you don't like her. You need try and hold her again. He shifted uncomfortably towards her, his knees hitting hers as he did so, which she responded to with a small yelp of pain.

"Ah, sorry! Are you okay?"

"Yeah, I'm fine; it wasn't that bad. I was just shocked, that's all."

She smiled at him in reassurance but he knew that she was hurt, both by the knees and by his accidental rejection of her advances. *Maybe they weren't advances though, maybe she was just cold or lonely.*

"Are you cold? If so we can move back to the Arena."

"Luke. It's boiling out here; the sun has only just gone down."

Oh god, now she thinks that I want to leave. Come on, Luke, get your head in the game, how is it that you can fight men with ease but struggle with physical contact with your best friend?

"I…I just wanted to check."

He awkwardly smiled at her, purposefully avoiding her eye contact. This time he just moved his hand towards hers, a subtle signal but one that he rested his hope in. He slowly slid it on the dirt ground, hoping she wouldn't notice just yet but he couldn't look at it to guide it otherwise it would be too obvious. This was a fatal error as he misjudged the distance and accidentally touched her hand, his fingertips lightly tapping hers. She moved her hand to take his but it was too late and he snatched his hand back up, humiliated. Two pale blue eyes were staring up at him and he had no idea what to do, so he just apologised and laughed it off, rubbing his neck as he did so. He felt so foolish. *If you had kept your hand there, she might have held it! She definitely thinks you're uninterested now.* All hope within Luke diminished as he sank into his shoulders and sighed loudly. She was still watching but the sigh seemed to really upset her. She got up and rubbed the dust off her clothes quite heatedly before telling him that she was tired and needed to go back.

Agnes left Luke alone in the field with the keys to his cage and his heart shattered. He strolled back to the Arena in misery, locked his cage, chucked the keys onto the floor outside and plodded onto the hard ground in a sulk. He had lost his chance with Agnes, and he felt like she'd hate him forever because of it. The night was long, sleepless and painful.

Art Part 5

It was just turning dusk as the eager pair watched the camp. Most of the tribe had similar features – dark skin, brown eyes, short hair and primitive clothing; however the arms that they carried were much more advanced, most probably taken from all the pirates that they had slaughtered over the years. But intermingled with them were women and men who looked much more like Art. They wore tattered but modern clothing and had light skin, which confused Art. He thought the tribe killed everyone that came to the island unwanted. As he looked closer though, he could see chain marks on their wrists and ankles, red raw wounds that looked fresh. *Maybe they're slaves or were, captured by pirates and then recaptured by these people.*

Kela was absently scratching her side with her teeth, waiting for the sun to set, curiously calm for the situation. Art on the other hand was a nervous wreck; his hands were sweaty as well as his brow and his toes twitched with agitation. During their journey to the camp, Art realised that he had caught the wrong end of the bargain and was now in a precarious situation. The plan couldn't be changed now but he was acutely aware of the dangers of his role in it.

Smoke rose high into the sky from the bonfires that marked the perimetre of the camp, blackening the sky that was otherwise clear and blue, although the blue was slowly being replaced with the night's dark purple hues. Stars began to appear and the moon was now visible but the day had not yet ended and the pair still had some time to wait before they could enact their plan that neither of them was certain would work. From the bushes that they were camped in, they could see all the goings-on in the tribe; the women washing clothes in a large pond at the centre of the encampment, the children play-fighting in the mud and the slaves dishing out refreshments and helping cook, clean and care for the tribe. The men were all either sharpening their weapons and tools or tending to the rows of crops that grew on the outskirts of the village. In many ways, they were like Art's people but steeped in a different culture and religion which, from what Kela had told him, was based around the storm that enveloped the island every few weeks. *I suppose their religion is just the same as ours, a hoax to keep people living the right way or maybe not a hoax and there actually is a grand deity out there. I don't want to find out just yet though; I want to live a little bit longer.* The two of them waited for the tribe to head to sleep before they began their plan.

Kela was the first to move, her body shrinking to the size of a pea and flying into the tents that that the tribe slept in. Art followed her lead and also began to move but in the opposite direction to find a good spot to make a distraction, which ended up being a hollow tree that must have been zapped by the storm as it was still slightly smouldering. From there, Art awaited Kela's signal.

He thought that the time for him to find a location would be enough time for Kela to awaken the tribe but she still hadn't given the signal after a few minutes of waiting. The blood pumping through Art's veins ran cold as he began to create scenarios in his head where Kela had been caught and eaten or tortured to reveal their plan or maybe she was on their side all along. It didn't take long for Art to panic but he kept to the plan and trusted Kela. *She needs me as much as I need her, so she won't betray me. I need to just follow the plan.* Amidst Art's panic, shouts echoed through the forest which did not help calm his nerves. A short few seconds later another sound boomed through the forest, a feral roar that shook Art and sent birds flying off their perches in the trees. *Was that the signal? It didn't sound like Kela but I can't think of anything else that could make a sound like that. It's certainly not human, that's for sure.*

"What are you doing, Art? I gave the signal," came Kela's voice inside art's head, although raspy and harsh.

Art instantly began bashing on the tree with a thick branch, sending deep concussive bangs through the forest. Shouts followed and the sound of feet running towards him came shortly after. Art continued to bash on the trunk though as he knew the tribe still had some distance to travel before they could get to him. The thuds reverberated into Art's skull, making him feel nauseous but he continued in spite of the feeling, to be absolutely sure that the hunters would not turn back. However, Art stayed far too long, only moving at the sight of red torches rapidly approaching. His first instinct was to run but he knew that he would be outpaced in seconds, so he climbed the nearest tree as high as he could and awaited the tribe's approach.

He was pleased with his pick of tree as the one he decided to climb was tall with numerous branches to clasp onto, making the ascent easy and somewhat silent. The fires didn't stop for long below the tree and continued onwards, only a few hunters stopping to look up into the foliage but the light of the torches couldn't illuminate far enough up for them to see Art, and they moved on relatively quick, not wanting to be separated from the herd in fear of the dark, just like Kela had said. Art breathed a sigh of relief, letting out a breath he hadn't realised he'd been holding and clambered back down the trunk, the descent slightly more challenging due to the absence of light except for the faint glow of the moon. When he finally hit the floor, he jogged back to the bushes the pair had watched from and waited for Kela's return.

He lay on the ground, thrilled by the success of the mission, even though it still wasn't quite over and watched as the tribe hectically paced their camp waiting for the hunters to return. To Art's dismay however Kela did not return and he couldn't spot her in the camp either. He searched, hawk-eyed for what seemed like hours until the hope inside of him began to fade but there was no sign of the bat.

Suddenly, huge gusts of air thumped Art's back, making him jump and squeak in distress and following that came two clangs just beside his frozen body. Staring down at Art was Kela, a huge grin on her face and a knife in her teeth. The boy was completely relieved at the sight of his new friend and the weapons lying beside him suggested that their plan was flawlessly successful without a hiccough. The shouts from inside the camp told a different story though.

"Let's not wait for them to find us. Hop on!"

Art did as he was told and hopped onto the giant bat's back, tightly clutching onto the weapons she had salvaged. Within seconds, they were soaring over the trees at lightning speed away from the tribe. Art did want to help the slaves but he had to stay alive first and live up to his promise to Kela, which in itself was a monumental task. *We've taken our first steps but I wish I wasn't here. I want the Captain to still be alive and to be back with my mother making sure she's getting better. I want to hold them again or at least see them once more.*

Kela after flying for a few minutes landed and caught her breath whilst Art checked out what she'd stolen. There was a knife, two cutlasses in sheaths and a large hunting spear, which Art was most attracted to. It allowed him to keep as much distance between himself and anyone trying to kill him.

"I hope I don't use these but they're handy. Thank you, Kela."

"No problem," she said between ragged breaths. "Phew, I'm out of breath and energy. I think I should return back to normal."

She didn't appear to be talking to Art but he vocalised his agreement with a hum, despite feeling like they weren't far enough away from the hunters yet. Kela's body once again began to convulse and she reduced her bulk to something more manageable, the original size that Art first met her in. Art was beginning to replay the events that had just transpired and began to wonder how Kela managed to make such a terrifying roar and why she didn't just use her telepathy as a signal. The boy absently rubbed his chin in thought, distracted from Kela's ramblings by his own internal monologue and completely oblivious to the fact that she had disappeared. A shuffling in some branches way above Art's head woke him from his daydreaming.

"Kela?"

"I'm here, you idiot, I just heard something that I'm going to investigate. I'll be back in a second, hang on."

Art couldn't spot her but he could hear her wings as she flapped away into the night in search of her hidden prey. Art decided not to waste time and picked up a cutlass, swinging it around awkwardly in an attempt to get used to its weight but he ended up dropping it on his foot and cutting himself. The wound wasn't bad, just a scratch but it did deter Art from using the sharp steel again. As a result, he picked up the spear and began to throw it from one hand to the other. It felt better than the sword but moving it around was just as awkward and tired his arms out considerably more, despite it being mostly wood except for a short, metal head with two small wings jutting out either side of it. It was definitely a weapon of practicality rather than showmanship and that comforted Art. He wanted the best and easiest weapon possible for his inexperienced and particularly weak hands. Despite the fatigue, Art lost himself to the flow of the weapon in the air, every articulation in his wrists making it move to his command. He rarely felt in control of anything but when holding the spear he felt strong and indomitable, like a hero of old, even if he was uneducated in any combat. In his peace, Art had forgotten all about Kela's departure and was utterly focussed on the ebb and flow of his body as he twisted, twirled and turned the spear.

After swinging the spear a few more times, Art gave in to the screaming muscles in his forearms and took a quick break, dropping to the floor and listening to the creatures of the night forage and hunt among the trees and bushes but as time passed Art also felt watched by some invisible presence. He swivelled around to check behind him for anyone and saw nothing, so he turned back to where he was facing and was met with a cutlass to his throat. Somehow the hunters had caught up with the renegade pair and found Art who was stunned by how fast they had hunted them down. He gulped, sweating profusely and shaking in fear. *Kela, where are you? Wherever you are, don't come back yet, they're here.* He was trying to contact her telepathically but with no luck. *I don't want to die yet, please.* More rustles from the treetops dragged the whole party's attention from Art to the canopy.

"Art? You there? I've caught myself some grub. Told you I heard something. Do you want…oh, that's not good."

Art was both pleased and dismayed that Kela was here. He didn't want her to get hurt but he didn't want to be alone either. He opened his mouth to speak but the cold steel pressed harder against his throat, stopping him from talking and opening a small wound that dribbled blood onto the blade. Kela took one look at the situation, shook her head and flew off without uttering another word. All compassion towards Kela in Art's heart was wiped clean. *That winged snake. Why would she leave me like this? Did I mean that little to her?* Art always relied on others and with such strong props like his mother and the Captain he was rarely disappointed, so this desertion stung.

It appeared the hunters could tell he was hurt and they laughed, which salted the wound. They had no empathy for outsiders, they were just killing machines. Art closed his eyes and waited to die at their hands. The blow never came but Art wished that it had.

Agnes Part 5

Three days had passed since Luke had broken Agnes's heart and she had been sour towards him ever since, avoiding him and ignoring him as best she could. She knew it was the wrong thing to do. She couldn't blame him for not liking her but it hurt to know he didn't reciprocate feelings. She wanted to forget about him but he was always in the back of her mind, an inescapable thought that pestered her constantly. Her love for him was boundless, which was why she wanted to fix the relationship she had severed and she was going to start doing that after the tournament that she was preparing to cheer him on for.

It was still early morning on day one of the tourney, so only a few fights had premiered but Kane and Luke were up next, facing a pair of gladiators from Eastern Europe who looked somewhat small compared to Lamorte's Taijitu. Despite the limited number of fights that had taken place, the dusty floor of the Pits was already bloodstained and gory, which made Agnes feel rather sick. She only wanted to watch Luke and Kane and she would be glad to be out of the stands and away from the stench of the Pits that came from both the pirates spectating and the defeated fighters lying lifeless on the ground. There were criminals from all across the globe, an overwhelming number from the Asian pirate trade routes who were an especially rowdy crowd but they were also rich and keen gamblers, so it wasn't all bad. Drinks were handed around by slaves, watered down by order of Lamorte to keep the pirates from getting too intoxicated and to save costs on the beverages. Lamorte himself was in a particularly good mood, drinking with the brigands and placing bets of his own on the fighters, which was mostly down to his profits from hosting the competition.

By the time Luke had to fight, the sun was high in the sky, roasting the spectators and gladiators alike, although in the private stands, there was shade so Agnes was shielded from the scorching rays. The pair of European fighters nervously walked out into the Pits, clearly untrained slaves that had been enlisted into the tourney either as punishment or for the amusement of their masters, in fact, Agnes felt pity on them. Luke and Kane however strode out into the Pits, playing off the clearly excited crowd. They wouldn't hold back against any opponent as they had been taught for years that any hesitation in this profession was fatal. The fight began with a bell from the side lines and was ended quickly with Luke throwing a javelin straight into the guts of one foe and Kane advancing on the other with a hand axe, chopping into his side like kindling. Agnes knew it would be over before it began but the audience seemed disappointed by the lack of entertainment. They wanted the boys to play with their food for a while.

Due to the speed of the first round of fights, the second round concluded the day, despite being planned for the next day. The untrained and weak fighters had all been cleaved from the line-up, so these fights were much more exciting and lengthier than the first, most of the fighters having to work hard to achieve victory. All except the Taijitu who finished off their enemy in a matter of moments. It was a gruesome affair but the buccaneers loved it, some of them already coinless because of gambling it all away but Agnes hated every minute of it. She was disgusted by the ruthlessness of it all but she didn't blame the fighters like Luke, they were all mostly slaves of the industry, so she focussed her abhorrence on the pirates that orchestrated the blood baths. But even then she knew some of them only did it because of the rewards of the trade, like Lamorte who she believed was also innocent. He was only playing his right cards to earn a more respectable living, even if it was slaughtering slaves to the pleasure of the crowds. He did appear to be enjoying himself but Agnes knew that deep down he was also sickened by the cold-blooded slayings and would stop it if it didn't mean financial ruin.

After Luke's fight, Agnes left the Arena to watch the setting of the sun. *I should congratulate him or something, at least show him that I care for him. Any day out there could be his last and I'm watching him put his life in danger without even wishing him good luck. Even if he doesn't love me, we're still friends and I need to show him but if I go there now I wouldn't be able to look him in the eye.* Agnes forgot about the sun, she was lost in her isolation and thoughts.

The next day was where the best fighters would clash to find the ultimate victors, the finishing of the second round and the beginning of the third round. Luke and Kane had fought their second round battle the day prior, so had the morning off to train and relax in their cages, and Agnes saw this as her opportunity to see them before they faced their toughest opponents yet. She bounded down the spiralling stairs to the cages, excited and giddy to see Luke again, and found them chatting together through the bars of their adjacent pens.

"You heard who we're fighting?"

"Yeah, Jack and Skall, from down the corridor," replied Kane.

"Don't know why they'd pin us up against another pair of Lamorte's fighters, it makes no sense."

"I doubt Lamorte will be having it though. He wants the greatest chance of winning and losing at least two of his fighters in one fell sweep isn't very good business."

"That's a fair point, let's wait and see what he does."

Agnes just sat and listened from the shadows, unsure of when to join in with the conversation. Just as she was about to jump in and participate, Kastas entered in a row.

"He's cancelling the fight!"

"What, Lamorte?" asked Kane.

"Yeah, he wants his pairs of fighters to fight another Captain's so that he doesn't lose out on the chance of winning."

"We were just talking about that," mentioned Luke "Although I don't see much of a problem,"

"Of course you don't, but the other Captains will definitely have something to say about it!"

"That's true. Lamorte winning is the one thing they don't want 'cause then they'll have to dish up even more money to the old miser," chuckled Kane.

"There's talk of rearranging the slots at random so that way there isn't any sour feeling towards the picks. It's just the luck of the draw."

That comment seemed to surprise Luke.

"Wait. I thought they were already random!"

"No, no. The Captains all come together and state their champions; in Lamorte's case, you two and then they're matched with easier opponents so that they all have a greater chance of winning. It's a good system until something like this happens."

"So what's wrong with a randomised line-up? Surely that's the next best thing?"

"You would think so but pirates aren't too fond of compromise, so they might make a big deal of this. And if they do, Lamorte is likely to get the brunt of the anger thrown his way, which means he'll then throw it at us."

Both Kane and Luke scratched their backs, *an odd coincidence*, Agnes thought, but it quickly escaped her mind as another of the crew came into the scene in a hurry holding a piece of paper. Kastas grabbed it off him and began to read aloud.

"The fight between Lamorte's two fighting pairs has been cancelled and the Asian pirate lord Lu-Feng has agreed to swap one of her fighter pairs with one of Lamorte's. Looks like you two will be fighting another of the pairs from Eastern Europe like you did in the first round while Jack and Skall must be fighting one of Lu-Feng's. I doubt you'll be seeing your training fellows again boys, that Asian pair are some of the best I've seen,"

"Shame, we don't get to face them," bragged Kane.

"Chances are you will."

Despite their bravado, the boys seemed slightly distressed by this. Even Agnes had heard the stories of the Asian fighters. They were nameless, slaves caught by the pirate lord in some remote village and trained from infants to deal death whenever their master deemed it fit. They had obliterated the

102

competition in silent determination, neither one of them sustaining any kind of wound whatsoever, which was remarkable given that they had already fought a pirate captain's champions in their second round. Agnes felt Luke and Kane's nerves but she had confidence that they would win.

She decided that in the silence she would walk in and wish them good luck and congratulate them but as she got up she fell and landed with a thud on the cold dirty stone floor. Both Kane and Kastas looked shocked but Luke just giggled. *He rejects me and then laughs at me...if those Asians don't kill him, I will.* She grimaced at him whilst being helped up by Kastas but by this point even he was laughing.

"I came to wish you good luck," she said with a smile, trying to play off the incident.

"Don't need it," remarked Kane, his ego restored.

"You need it more than you know," commented Kastas.

"Thank you," responded Luke, although slightly late. He even added a smile to make it seem more sincere, which made Agnes melt.

His goofy smile through the bars tore away her hate for the brute's actions and she fell for him once again, literally falling head over heels.

"Well, I guess I should leave you boys to it then, don't want to interfere."

She slowly backed away but was stopped by a hand on her shoulder. It was the Captain. He looked down on her with curiosity, his usual smile at seeing her absent from his face. It was instead replaced with a stern frown but it wasn't aimed at her, in fact she couldn't tell who it was aimed at.

"Ahh, Agnes, thought you'd be here. Bringing food for my champions? Yes, good. I need to speak with these three privately, is it okay if you leave for a while?"

Normally Agnes would have refused but his unpleasant demeanour worried her and she left without hesitation. It surprised her to see such a jolly man in a bad mood, she rarely saw him show any emotion other than sad or happy, both normally a result of alcohol. She did however turn as she left and caught Luke's eye, quickly looking away and walking back up the stairs, catching only the start of the conversation.

"You two need to win this tournament because I'm."

His voice faded as Agnes strolled away.

The Captains' lounge in the Arena was bustling with activity. There were captains from all over the world betting, drinking and talking business to the ambience of men slaughtering each other for entertainment. Agnes was one of the only women in the entire hall and it showed. As she walked past the men, they would stare at her and cat call, some even daring to get close enough to touch her but Lamorte was often there to save her. However, for the moment he was with Luke, Kane and Kastas, so her senses were heightened in fear. She could feel eyes on her, watching her like a predator stalks its prey. Conversations often stopped when she passed a table, the desperate men thieving for some contact with the closest woman they could find, which was her. Some of them had brought in their own private female slaves but to those that didn't they had no one to grope and Agnes was fair game to them, even if she was under Captain Lamorte's protection. She made her way through the ranks of rancid breath, drunks and cheap liquor, heading towards a table close to the window so that she could watch Luke but she was held back by one of the men.

"Come, talk to me a while, princess. I promise not to bite. Unless of course that's what you want."

He over-exaggerated a wink and began to pull her close to him. He was clearly drunk, his eyes squinted and his speech slurred but that only made him harder to break away from. Agnes tried to pull back but the man was too strong and managed to haul her onto his lap and hold her there, despite her obvious discomfort. The other pirate captains just watched as the man put one of his hands onto Agnes's breast and caressed it, she wanted to puke. Carefully tracing his other hand on her thigh, the man began to make his way up her leg, which lit a fire in Agnes and she began bucking and writhing to get out of his grip. But it was no use, he was too strong.

Then, all of a sudden out of nowhere a dagger was at the man's throat, the point as close to his skin as possible without perforating it.

"I think that's enough. Don't you?"

The voice was a woman's, soft and charming but full of detest. The man didn't even speak; he just pushed Agnes off his lap and held up his hands in defeat. Agnes was especially glad too, as the man had pissed himself in panic.

"Follow me," the woman said to Agnes.

Without waiting for a response, she turned and walked towards a table overlooking the Pits and sat, not even looking at Agnes. This mysterious woman was covered in exotic jewellery and clothing, a hint towards vast wealth, and had long, black hair that trailed behind her, its length reaching her waist. She had almond shaped eyes and pale skin but her lips were a vibrant red, matching her red cloak. Agnes could see why the man didn't argue. This woman was fierce.

"I'm Lu-Feng, Pirate Lord of Asia. I would offer you to sit but you seem to have already made yourself comfortable."

"Oh, I'm sorry, I didn't mean to offend you, I thought."

"Don't worry," she interrupted. "Just remember next time, it's bad manners to sit before your host sits."

Agnes hadn't noticed it before but the pirate had a strange articulation that made her speech all the more elegant.

"You're a pirate?"

"I'm offended by your doubts. But I'm not like this scum, so I understand your confusion and I'll let the insult slide."

"I'm sorry, it's just."

"I'm a woman? Yes, it often surprises people. But aren't you a pirate?"

"Me? Oh, no. I didn't think girls were allowed to be."

"Darling, this is piracy, there aren't any rules. I can be whatever I want in this business."

I didn't think about it that way.

"Well? Are you going to tell me your name? I find it quite rude not to know my guest's name."

"Agnes," she meekly replied.

"Agnes what?"

"Agnes."

"Ahh, Lu-Feng! I see you've made acquaintances with Agnes here. I hope she hasn't been too much trouble," Lamorte shouted from a few metres away, winking at Agnes and smiling.

"Oh, no, she's quite a pleasure to speak with. It's these randy delinquents here that're driving me crazy. One of them nearly had Agnes."

"Who?"

Lamorte's smile evaporated in an instant and he flushed red in rage. Feng just pointed at the man that had harassed Agnes just moments before. He drew his sword and stabbed the man straight through the stomach, twisting the blade to the cries of his agonised victim. The man died in pain and Agnes wasn't even fazed. She almost felt pleased.

"Let that serve as a warning to any of you that also try and touch Agnes!"

Lamorte spat as he shouted, the room falling dead quiet for a few long seconds before returning back to its usual clamour. The Captain returned, still red in the face but without the frenzied, wrathful look in his eyes.

"No lack of subtlety with you, Lamorte," Lu-Feng added sarcastically.

The captain just shot her a look of discontent at the retort.

"Thanks for helping her, Feng," he muttered.

"I see she means a lot to you, I wonder why that is."

The anger once again flooded into Lamorte's face but he quickly diminished it knowing that an attack on another Pirate Lord would mean war between the factions. Agnes herself wanted to scream out the answer so that everyone would know and she wouldn't have to keep it a secret anymore. She didn't because Lamorte didn't want people to know and she respected him, loved him even and wouldn't want to hurt him like that.

"I understand," continued Lu-Feng. "We all have secrets we don't want to be shared."

The lady turned her head to Agnes and smiled, a nice sight on a face that so far had been monotonous and bland.

"I am also grateful to you for allowing our fighters to swap."

"Oh, that's not a problem because I'll be winning anyways."

She turned her smile towards Lamorte but it lost sincerity and gained a sense of mockery, which didn't help to soothe the Captain's anger.

"I'm glad you're confident, Feng. Makes it all the more fun to watch you lose."

"You don't need false bravado around me, Lamorte, I'm much more civilised than that."

Art Part 6

Art was encaged within a small mud hut that had barred windows and a barricaded door. It stank of faeces and death, what Art thought was the legacy of the building's previous inhabitants and its thatch roof was in complete disregard, the holes filled in with wooden planks and tar. No one had visited Art for the entire two days he had been captive; it was as though he were in some kind of isolated prison like Bedlam. The only hint of outside life was the bread and meat scraps he was fed through a gap in the door and the water trough sitting outside the hut that he could drink from by a hand-sized hole in the wall.

The night's cold air had seeped into Art's bones and he was shivering uncontrollably to try and dispel the chill that was consuming him. Deep grunts and chants could be heard from the centre of the village, the tribes people all joining in with what Art could only presume was some kind of religious or cultural ceremony. But through the windows he couldn't see it which he was glad for to some extent. *They could be sacrificing animals or their slaves or something; I think it's for the better that I can't see.*

Art's mind often wandered to Kela and each time it did he grew angrier. To him she was a scandalous traitor that had betrayed him for her own safety, despite calling on him to help her with her scheme and calling him friend. When he needed her most, she abandoned him without hesitation. He knew, however, that if the roles were reversed he probably would have done the same but it still hurt none the less. He wasn't a hero. He had always left that job to Captain Lamorte but now that he was gone, the spot was empty, yet Art didn't feel he had the right to fill those shoes. When Art thought of the Captain, he thought of strength and valour but when he pictured himself, all he saw was weakness and fear, a boy that doesn't have a reason for existing. It's not that he wanted to die, it was just he didn't have a purpose in life.

Three loud bangs startled Art and knocked him out of his daydreaming. The face that appeared at the door was unfamiliar to Art, which frightened him considerably. It was quite pig-like with a large round nose and squinted eyes and the body attached to it was just as hideous with scars and tattoos covering his skin so that there was almost nothing human left, just ink and thick, pink scars. He opened the door, advanced on Art and grabbed him by the collar of his ragged shirt, pulling him out of the hut and into the night.

The air was warmer out in the open than in the primitive hut but Art was still cold. He looked around anxiously at the faces that had stopped to look at the strange, white-skinned intruder they had captured. Some children were even there, mocking him for some reason or another in a language that Art had never heard before, although their parents didn't seem impressed by the comments made. He was hauled viciously through the rows of people towards a huge, flaming pit that had been decorated with the skulls of all kinds of invertebrates but most notably human. As he was brought nearer to the pit, the hunters began to chant once more, much to the dismay of Art who was now struggling to get out of the man's vice-like grip and fearing for his life. First the chants were slow and lethargic but gradually they began to increase in speed and volume until the whole village was filled with the echoes of the deep, violent grunts and hums that shook the surrounding forest. Art was in serious trouble.

Torches suddenly lit the path that Art had walked down as well as three other paths that also led to the sacrificial fire pit. Walking down those paths were three other captives; slaves to the tribe that had outlived their welcome and were now to be sacrificed with Art. Only one of them was female but she was heavily pregnant with trails of blood flowing down her legs from her crotch. Art guessed that the tribe had already taken care of the baby. Her sobs were now audible to Art, although his heart was also beating loud and fast, echoing in his head but by far the most deafening sound was the bloodcurdling chant of the tribe. Art looked to his right at another of the slaves and saw that he had soiled himself, the children of the tribe finding it hysterical. What scared Art the most was the expressions on the hunters' faces. They were all smiling but maliciously, ear to ear grins that sent shivers down Art's spine. It was as though they were all part of one entity, simultaneously shouting to the beat of drums coming from inside one of the caves protruding into the cliffs.

He was dragged closer to the roaring flames. The heat became a sudden explosion on his chest as he drew close enough to smell the burning logs fuelling the great fire. It wasn't painful just yet but the march of the man dragging him continued and slowly the heat began to evolve into a slight burn, which was when the man stopped and put Art in front of him. Another hunter handed him a spear that the man used to prod Art ever forward into the sweltering abyss, the head of the spear piercing the skin on his back when he attempted to pull away. Art yelped in pain, both from the spear and the fire. His skin began to sear, first the hairs on his arms and legs but eventually his whole body began to burn. Screams from all four of the captives filled the air. One last push and Art was falling into the fiery pit.

Luke Part 7

Luke watched Captain Lamorte leave, making sure he was well beyond earshot before resuming his conversation with Kastas and Kane.

"What do you think?" he asked Kane.

"It's fine. No matter who we fight we'll win. We've got nothing to worry about with his threats. He's only threatening us because he himself feels threatened by Lu-Feng. The pair has a lot of feats to back up their strength though, so I think it will be as close a fight as you can get against us two."

"Well, it is somewhat nice to hear that you care for your lives, even if you do live in ungracious dog holes owned by a man with more care for shit under his boots than you two. You and these other fighters are both undefeated, so it's safe to say that this will be the fight the whole Arena will want to see. Never mind that though, you've got another fight before that, so worry about the European pair first."

With that Kastas left. Luke turned to Kane with a huge grin on his face, his friend also beaming.

"We'll win this next one easy, so let's move on with the conversation, which is useful as I had something I want to tell you."

"Agnes?"

Luke's eyes widened in fear and he turned around frenziedly.

"What? Where?"

"No, you moron, I was asking if it was about Agnes."

"Oh. Haha. Yes, it is how'd you know?"

"Only two things make you smile like that. Food and Agnes."

"No arguments here." He laughed. "Anyways, we had a moment!"

"Like a falling out moment or a romantic moment," asked Kane, genuinely curious.

"Why would I be smiling if it were a falling out moment?"

"I'm just getting context."

"Surprised you know that word. But that's not the point; the point is that I ruined a romantic evening by hitting Agnes."

"Whoa! Bit extreme, don't you think?"

"Oh, shit no, not like that. As in I moved and accidentally hit her with my leg."

The conversation was halted by one of the crew walking in.

"You two are fighting next, get ready," he shouted from a little way down the corridor, promptly leaving straight after unlocking their cages.

"Yeah, okay, and what else?" Kane prompted as they walked up the spiralling stairs to the Pits.

"Well, we sat down talking and watching the sunset."

"Hold on, how'd that happen? Thought you're only allowed in the Pits at night?"

"Oh. She unlocked my cage."

Kane looked slightly jealous of the freedom but continued walking. They opened the huge, iron gate into the Pits and walked out onto the dusty ground to the cheers of countless drunken pirates.

"Good on you, I would've escaped."

Luke ignored the comment and continued with his story whilst picking up a cutlass from the ground. Kane found two daggers and used them instead.

"She got closer to me and actually held my hand but I wanted to wipe the sweat off so it wouldn't be slippery or uncomfortable for her. Thing is, I didn't know whether it would be weird if I picked it back up again."

"Tell me you did. If you didn't, you'll be fighting me as well."

"I didn't."

"You're an idiot. What else went wrong 'cause from a start like that I can't imagine the night went well."

They took a quick break to scope out the competition. The two enemy fighters were both of average height and build and seemed to hold a blade with relative skill, so Luke began to devise a plan of attack with Kane.

"You flank right, I'll take the centre and push my guy towards you so that we can take them two on two if you haven't killed yours by that point."

"Got it. Now continue the story because I'm captivated mister lover boy."

They both began to advance on their foes, Kane veering off right and Luke ploughing on forwards.

"Well, I put my hand down beside hers which changed my position and she took her head off my shoulder."

Luke's man jumped at him but Luke parried the attack with little effort.

115

"She did the leaning thing! Wow, she really likes you man!"

Luke countered with a huge slash of his cutlass that was also blocked but it did push the fighter back and to the right just as Luke wanted.

"I hope so."

"Well, she might not be after you being an idiot. Oh, well, what then?"

Kane was also engaged in battle, the steel clashes from his two knives ricocheting off the walls of the Arena and echoing all around so that it sounded like a thousand battles rather than just one.

"That's when I hit her in the knee with my legs as I changed position."

Luke continued pressing forward with attack after attack, closing the distance between him and Kane. Most of the slashes were blocked or dodged but a couple grazed his shoulder or chin. The man already looked terrified.

"It probably hurt too," he added.

"I wonder why," Kane shouted between breaths, his opponent proving to be a little more challenging than Luke's.

Luke's adversary was going on the counter but due to Luke's massive size he made no progress and ended up being put on the back foot once more.

"Yeah, not a great move but it gets worse, don't worry."

"That doesn't surprise me!" Kane laughed in between strikes.

By this point, Luke had managed to push his opposition all the way to the edge of the Pits where Kane was fighting and they began to attack in unison, one hacking away whilst the other blocked.

"So then I moved my hand towards hers to try and hold it again."

"A last ditch attempt."

"Exactly."

Luke sliced at his opponent, opening up a huge gash in his stomach that splashed blood into Luke's face as the guts fell out and slopped to the floor. The man let out a squeal and sank to the ground.

"Could you hurry up and finish yours, I've already done mine!"

"Not until you finish the story but some help might be nice!"

Luke was planning on just watching his friend but decided that helping would get the gruesome work done quicker.

"Well, anyways, I moved my hand a bit too far and accidentally tapped hers."

"Accidently. Right," Kane added sarcastically. "Did she hold it though?"

"Well, she did try too but I had already pulled my hand away in embarrassment by that point."

Kane threw a dagger at the fighter, killing him instantly with the blade piercing through one of his eyes and embedding itself in his skull.

"What! Oh, for god's sake. You really are a moron."

He turned to face Luke with a face of pure hysterics. *Seems he's as irritated as me.* Suddenly the sounds of cheers and shouts flooded into Luke's head, the celebrations of those that had bet on the pair to win. For a moment, Luke forgot that he was in the Pits and had been ignoring the crowd the whole fight but with it all now over he was aware once more.

"There's no excuse for that, really mate, you completely messed it up."

"Thanks for the reminder, Kane."

Kane clutched his stomach and laughed into the air at Luke's obvious shame.

"I don't want to rub it in but…"

"Yes, you do! Don't lie."

"Okay, maybe a bit but come on! You've liked that girl for years and yet as soon as you get close to her you're a shambles. You two have spent the better part of eight years together. You should have just told her rather than fumbled around like an idiot."

"And suddenly you're an expert?"

Kane didn't respond, he just raised his eyebrows and smiled and then turned to the crowd that had somewhat died down. He raised his arms in triumph and pumped a fist into the sky, slowly bringing the spectators' excitement back up. Luke decided not to celebrate the victory, instead he walked out of the pits and wiped the sweat off his brow with a rag he found on the benches. There he waited for Kane to get bored of the stardom and together they made their way back to their cages where Kastas was waiting.

The old man was fast asleep on the chair just outside Luke's cage, the same one that Agnes had sat on all those years ago when Hal had gotten injured. He was clearly having a good dream as he was smiling jovially and mumbled every-so-often. Luke and Kane took the break to also have a nap, recuperating their energy before the final match. They had no idea who it would be against but Jack and Skall hadn't returned from the Pits for quite some time, so Luke thought it safe to assume that he and Kane would be fighting the Asian fighters next. Their prestige scared him but he was also impressed by their record. When push came to shove, Luke wasn't sure he would be on the winning side.

Art Part 7

Fire had enveloped Art, the flames licking his skin as they danced in the night. Art screamed until his lungs were burning from the smoke, heat and hyperventilation, the pain flashing throughout his body like a thunderbolt striking him down. The few seconds he had spent in the blaze felt like an eternity in hell but as time went on he grew confused. The others that had also been sacrificed were all but ash now but he was still being tortured. He glanced down at his body and saw no harm had come to him, he felt the agonising explosions of pain but his skin was still fair and smooth. *I am already in Hell.* He began to cry as well as scream, his thoughts resting on his mother and Captain Lamorte who were the last two people to love Art. The tears were scorched off his face.

Yells from above him caught his attention. Through the intense amber glow Art couldn't make out a thing other than the fact that he was alone in the pit and someone was trying to get at him. Then out of the blue, a huge flow of water was thrown over his head, dousing the spiralling flames with a spitting hiss. The feeling of relief was euphoric. However, the turn of events had heightened Art's bewilderment and he wasn't entirely sure he wanted to know what was going to happen to him next.

He licked some of the water off of his forearm hoping to quench his thirst but it was salty and tasted revolting so he immediately spat it back out again. Then it dawned on him. *That's sea water, how did that much get this far inland? Surely, no man could carry a load that size.*

"I am no man!"

"Kela," he whispered.

Then, as if on cue he was clasped by two giant feet that whisked him into the night sky and away from the awe-struck natives that stood watching the duo escape. They hurried towards the side of the island that Art had not yet been to, the forest much thinner here and scattered with human settlements and outposts. A couple of them were much larger than the one by the mountain but still not even a fraction of the size of London. Other than the fires that outlined the tribe's habitations, the island was dark and eerie, the only sounds being that of insects and nocturnal birds, much quieter than the other side of the island. Art assumed that the lack of life was due to the human inhabitants, as well as the forest's much thinner canopy. *Humans take wherever they are and rarely give back. What is our place on this planet?* The combination of the wind pounding against his face and his mind's fondness for daydreaming stole Art's concentration but he eventually became conscious of the situation when he and Kela landed in a small clearing that was covered by thick boughs and branches from humongous trees whose fruit was bright red like an apple but much larger and spikier. Kela was smiling down upon her human companion with a pride-filed grin but Art was not best pleased with her.

"Why'd you come back?" he uttered quite bluntly.

"What do you mean? Of course I came back for you. That is what friends are for, right?"

"I suppose so."

"Oh, good, I wasn't quite sure. Haven't had a friend in a few centuries you see."

"I thought you abandoned me."

"Don't be ridiculous, I need you," she hollered with a beaming smile.

"Well, thanks, but if you don't mind me asking, HOW AM I NOT DEAD?"

"Oh, that was me too. It did use up most of my magic store though, so don't get captured again for a while."

"Wait, so it was all you? The protection from the flames, the water. All you?"

"Technically it was the magic but, yes, it was me."

"Wow."

"We have a mission still though, so let's get working on that. Grab this and we'll make for the other side of the mountain."

Kela handed him a spear and Art firmly grasped it with both hands, swinging it slightly before continuing the conversation.

"Why the other side?"

"I was scouting whilst you were captured and realised that the opening to the stairs that'll lead us up to where the crystal is isn't anywhere near the village, in fact it's the opposite side of the mountain, so that's where we are headed."

"That's good news then. If the tribe don't see or hear us, then we only have to deal with the monsters from the storm."

"And they're only active during a storm, so as long as we're not caught out, we should be able to walk in, destroy the crystal and leave without anyone or anything noticing."

"Things are looking up."

Secretly Art was sceptical about the plan but he knew that both his and Kela's hope was running thin and they needed a victory.

"On second thoughts, I think we should eat and sleep first," admitted Kela, her stomach rumbling in response.

And with that the two of them settled, Art under a tree and Kela dangling upside down on one of its branches. They slept until the rising of the sun.

Agnes Part 6

Fireworks screamed into the sky and exploded in a beautiful array of vibrant colours that dazzled the pirate audience who gawked at the great flashes of light. The day's events had ended and the sun had set, leaving the pirates to party and gamble under the specially built parasols that were fenced in and guarded under order of the Captain. Agnes was very much against attending but Lamorte insisted, so she changed into a more lady-like summer dress and was forced to interact with the drunks that had nothing but women and money on their minds. They looked her up and down wherever she went and she felt uncomfortable the whole time because of it. However, to her gladness, Lamorte had organised a small protectorate to stop any unwanted interactions made of members of the crew and the Captain's personal slave Hal. He seemed happy to get away from the Captain. *Poor boy, no wonder he's tired of Lamorte's shit, I get exhausted just being around him for a couple of minutes. I could scarcely imagine what eight years would do to you.* She got her response in Hal's avoidance of any other human contact; in fact he hardly even looked at her unless he was passing her a drink. He stayed clear of her and let her mind her own business, which made certain that she had to make conversation with someone else.

She gradually began searching for Lu-Feng but the pirate queen was not there, so she resorted to sitting with a small group of British privateers who seemed the least dubious out of the collection of thieves, bandits and private sailors. They were nice enough, letting her sit and eat with them but their conversation was less than interesting to Agnes; like all boys they were talking about pugilism, politics and boats. The crew assigned to protect her seemed just as jaded from the dull discourse, so she let them disperse because she was sure that after Lamorte's show of anger earlier that day, nobody was going to get anywhere near her, especially with the Captains personal slave prowling in the shade watching like a hawk.

Finally, after at least a couple hours of the dreary dialogue, the fighters were brought in with Luke in tow. The pirate hoard encircled them as they began to train as additional entertainment for the intoxicated buccaneers. Most of them were injured from the fights or too young to compete but Kane, Luke and the Asian pair were unscathed and made it their goal to boast the others into submission. They showed their skill with each of the weapons on hand and the pirates loved it but Agnes could tell that Kane and Luke were just kidding around and pretending to look serious so as to fool the Asian fighters into thinking that this was how they fought in battle. In reality, the boys were using basic techniques and average form to throw them off when it came to the real fight. It seemed to be working too, as the undefeated fighters looked completely unimpressed by Luke and Kane's show. *One of Kastas's schemes for sure. For an old man, he's sly as a fox.*

Agnes got up off her seat, thanked the privateers and made her way towards Luke who had by this point lost his crowd and was watched solely by Lu-Feng's fighters and Kastas, other than quick glances from distracted pirates. She didn't want to speak to Luke, so she just stood and watched but it looked like she'd put him off as he was completely off balance and wouldn't stop gazing at her. She blushed at the attention.

The night concluded when the fighters had left, the liquor had run dry and the pirates had all made for their ships.

The next day was much slower to start than the day previous, mostly due to the intense hangovers that they'd all procured from the night's drinking as well as the day's for most of them. Agnes herself wasn't hung over, she was too nervous to drink excessively, even if she wanted to. By the afternoon, however, things were in full swing and the show had begun. For the last day of events, Lamorte had organised fights between animals from all across the globe and they were the goriest by far with starved creatures tearing each other limb from limb and devouring the numerous carcasses scattered around the Pits before being killed and eaten themselves. The only animal not to die was the elephant that the crew had caught a month prior from the local savannah but it did suffer huge gouges and bite-marks all over its massive body, most of them from the Bengal tiger that the British privateers had brought along. The most impressive fight however was that of two dog packs, one from East Asia and the other from Europe, both with around eight members of different species. They went at each other with an intense ferocity that Agnes had never seen before, and after a gruelling fight, not a single hound was still breathing, much to the dismay of those that had bet on either side. These fights meant nothing to Agnes. She was only interested in Luke's fight.

She was sat, much like the day before, between Lu-Feng and Lamorte and watched the ensuing fights from high above the Pits in the Captains' suite, which she was glad for, because after three days of drinking and brawling, the stands had begun to reek and the Pits were no better. It was about two in the afternoon by the time the tournament finale went underway and Agnes couldn't wait for it to end and she could be sure that Luke would be safe.

Warm air flowed into the Arena, the breeze doing nothing to mitigate the intense heat that burned down on the spectators. The morning had only been warm but with the sun now high in the sky and heading west it was scorching. Agnes was grateful for the cold stone ceiling of the Captains' suite but she still felt the heat excruciatingly when the fighters entered the Pits; their passion burned much deeper than any of the sun's sizzling waves, and from what Agnes could tell, the rest of the Arena could feel it too. Unlike normal, Kane and Luke were silent and cautious, mirroring the opposing fighters who stood still as statues staring down their competition and putting everybody on edge. When the bell rang to signal the start of the match, however, they sprang to life and darted towards the central weapons rack where they each grabbed a strange looking two-handed sword, whereas Kane and Luke grabbed weapons that were already on the ground, the selection there being much more limited but there weren't many weapons that Agnes hadn't seen them train with. Kane had a long, bloodied spear but Luke had only managed to find two bucklers which he'd strapped precariously to his fists. It was there that they waited for the Asian fighters to advance.

Noise in the Arena began to rise once more as the pirates cheered on their champions but the silence lingered in the Pits until Lu-Feng's fighters burst into action and charged on Luke and Kane, shouting curses or prayers, Agnes couldn't tell. Luke and Kane began smiling. Just as the fighters collided, they changed stances and position with Luke at the front and Kane at the back, pointing his spear at the fighters so that they couldn't advance any further without being skewered which kept him and Luke safe from any close-ranged attacks. Step by step the two of them began their own charge, pushing the others back towards the rack. But these were experienced fighters and quickly adapted their strategy, each of them moving to a separate side of Luke so that Kane's spear could only focus on one at a time. This prompted Luke and Kane's next move which was to lure the two fighters to two separate corners of the Pits in order to ensure that they couldn't team up against one but that meant that Luke and Kane were completely alone in their respective areas and vulnerable to attacks. It seemed the other fighters were pleased with this new arrangement as they too were smiling now but more akin to feral beasts.

Agnes wanted to watch both fights at the same time but due to the distance between them she could only concentrate on one, so she first turned to Luke's battle and watched intently, flinching at every strike. Luke had planted his feet and was parrying and blocking blow after blow from the Asian fighter who fought with a unique chaos and speed that blurred his moves so that the only way Agnes knew Luke was safe was from the metallic twang from the sword hitting his small round shields. The fighter was clearly using trained techniques, whereas Luke was relying on his intuition, as bucklers were an unusual weapon to dual-wield at the best of times. He seemed to be in his element, however, the much smaller fighter's attacks never breaking his indomitable defence and it was only a matter of time before Luke went on the offensive himself. For the moment, though he was biding his time and analysing his enemy just as Kastas had taught him over the years. The opposing fighter was obviously getting enraged at his ineffectiveness and threw a huge overhead strike at Luke, straying from his pattern of side slashes, which caught Luke off-guard as he must have also fallen into a pattern. In an effort to keep the blade from slicing him in two, Luke caught the sword between both his bucklers but that did little to reduce the power of the blow and the shining steel glided through his grip and cut a long red line across Luke's muscular chest from collar bone to naval. He grunted in pain but to Agnes's relief as well as his own, the wound had not penetrated completely through his hide-like skin and had only nicked the surface. The startled combatant jumped back and recollected himself before running at the Asian fighter and beginning his own chain of vicious attacks in protest.

The first few swings were masterfully blocked but as Luke began to break the other fighter's guard he rolled away and dodged a punch that otherwise would have been fatal. With Luke off balance from the attack, the fighter took his chance and slashed his blade across Luke's back, running opposite to the previous gash across his chest, this hit had no effect on Luke however, and he ended up laughing when he turned to see the fighter's shocked expression. The attack, despite its force, hardly even scratched Luke's thick, scar-coated back and only sent a small trickle of blood down

Luke's enormous torso. Agnes had seen the scars inflicted on Luke from the whippings and she wasn't surprised that his back had become stone from how brutal and numerous they had been. Luke then resumed his rush and continued battering the fighter with his bucklers the first few once again being blocked with immense aptitude but Luke's punches were so crushing that they began to bend the strange looking sword until it snapped completely, garnering several cheers from the audience and a look of pure dread on Lu-Feng's champion. With this, Luke stopped his attack and lifted the opposing fighter off the ground where he had fallen from the sheer power of the blows in an attempt to act honourable but the fighter took the opportunity to stab his broken blade deep into Luke's thigh. He screamed in pain and fell the ground, grabbing his leg and falling to one knee.

The fighter showed Luke his broken sword, the blood dripping off it thick and dark red, and pulled it back to finish his job. Agnes screamed in horror as the blade came plummeting down towards Luke but Luke jumped up into the fighter and tackled him to the ground, his agonised screams only a ploy to put the Asian fighter off guard. Luke with his arms wrapped around the fighter released his grip and began to pound at the fighter's head with his iron clad fists. Blood squirted out of his nose and eyes and teeth flew in all directions. The man was dead but Luke didn't stop and to ensure his victory, he thrust a buckler into the fighter's neck, perforating his skin and causing great gouts of blood to come streaming from the dead man's throat. Agnes breathed a sigh of relief and turned to see Kane being held by the scruff of the neck, about to be skewered by his opponent's blade. Luke also saw him dangling in the fighter's grasp and screamed in desperation.

In a frantic attempt to save his best friend, Luke threw one of his bucklers at the opponent who was still preparing to strike. The metal plate soared through the air and crashed into Kane's chest but managed to slice into the other fighter's hand. Both of them bellowed in pain and Kane was dropped onto the ground in a heavy heap. Luke's buckler had knocked the air out of him completely and he lay sprawled across the ground winded and gasping for air. The other fighter however had re-gathered his strength and concentration, and was once again rearing back to impale Kane. In follow up to his monstrous throw, Luke ran at the Asian fighter to continue protecting his friend. He reached him just in time to stop him from sinking his blade into Kane's stomach.

Luke barged into him with incredible force, so much that Agnes heard something snap inside the fighter's back, which produce an inaudible scream from the Asian fighter who was now also on the ground with Luke standing on top of him in a deadly rage. He was panting heavily and bleeding copiously from his wounds, his leg wound spurting thick blood onto the dirt floor. The brute of a man collapsed on the ground next to Lu-Feng's last champion who had yet to move. Time ticked on and the three men had still not moved other than Kane writhing on the ground and clasping his chest where the buckler had collided with him. Agnes couldn't tell if either of the others were alive and from the commotion in the Captain's suite and the rest of the Arena, neither could the other spectators.

The cold stone of the Arena was aglow with the golden aura of the blistering sun. Under the amber rays, the blood looked almost black as it pooled around Luke and the other fighter and from what Agnes could tell, the crimson ichor was from both of the fighters' numerous wounds. She looked on in horror as the man she had grown to love more than anything bled to death as entertainment for the pirates that she had called kin for as far back as her memory could take her. She looked around her. They were all unfazed, some even laughing at the tragedy that was unfolding before them; she was utterly disgusted and more ashamed than she felt was possible. In that moment, she realised the true nature of pirates and it chilled her to the bone. Then sudden cheers broke out amongst them as they watched the fight come to its grizzly conclusion. Agnes clenched her fists and her vision clouded red as she flew into a fit of such ferocious fury that she began to attack those around her. She was so blinded by her hate that she didn't see Luke rise of the ground and sink the Asian fighter's own blade into his stomach. When she finally realised what had happened, she had knocked two surprised captains unconscious and was holding one of them in a head-lock.

Luke looked up at her and they locked eyes. She slowly released the pirate, the energy in her arms sinking away and ran towards the window of the suite with tears uncontrollably streaming down her face. They had won. They were safe. Agnes didn't have to worry anymore.

Luke Part 8

The Arena was roaring with cheers and shouts. Luke felt feint and nauseous, the blood seeping out of his wounds at an alarming rate, and his leg throbbed with a consistent ache that pounded in rhythm with his heart. His vision was slowly becoming clouded but he still went to go check on Kane who had managed to also get to his feet and was making his way towards Luke. They embraced each other, despite the pain that came soaring through each of them when they squeezed too hard. They were both fine for the time being but Luke could feel his strength fading and wasn't sure he'd be able to make it much longer. He broke away from Kane and made his way towards the side of the Pits where Kastas met him with bandages and alcohol to help with his injuries. The last he remembered was falling heavily into Kastas's arms.

He awoke suddenly, his body sweating profusely and convulsing in agony. His wounds were all bandaged up and cleaned but they still leaked blood and other fluids that gradually soaked through the clean dressing on his wound. Heat swam in through the open window of the infirmary yet Luke felt cold as ice and began shivering uncontrollably, which made Kastas pull a short, stained linen blanket over him but it did little to impede the chill. His whole body ached and burned and he felt like death itself. Soon after attempting to move he lost consciousness again.

His eyes opened groggily as great long streams of light filtered through the window straight onto Luke's bed but he was grateful for its warmth and the energy it helped renew inside him. He felt much better than he did previously, the pains subsiding into slight itches and aches but they were manageable. This time when he tried to sit up, his body didn't give way and he could finally stretch out his taut muscles. The room around him was small and unorganised but had a sense of homeliness about it, although Luke put that down to the fact that he hadn't been in a home for a very long time. Nobody was in there except for Luke and he was thankful that he could have some peace, especially since his head was spinning in every which way, making him dizzy. Drowsiness soon took him and he lay back down and slept.

Voices awoke him from his slumber and he recognised them instantly; it was Lamorte and Agnes, the one whom Luke hated the most and the one whom he loved the most. They were discussing some trivial topic that Luke didn't focus on too much as his head still hurt, although the rest of his body was much livelier. Finally he opened his eyes and turned towards the two speakers who were so involved in their own conversation that they must have forgotten Luke was there, as they looked surprised to see him awake. Agnes was the first to react by helping Luke sit up whilst Lamorte looked on and she held on to him for quite a while, feigning that she was helping him but Luke could tell she just wanted to hold him even if the Captain was right there. Lamorte himself even got up and grabbed Luke's arm in some kind of warrior's embrace but he didn't hold it for long and went straight back to sitting on his chair.

"How are you feeling?" asked Agnes, clearly worried for him.

Luke only nodded.

"That's good, my boy," butted Lamorte. "You fought well and I thank you for your service. I was very worried about you for a moment there; I couldn't lose my top champion, could I?"

He laughed at his own little joke and got up to leave the room but Agnes pulled him back down. Luke was shocked to see him acting so submissive and kind.

"Oh, of course, I nearly forgot. I would like reward you with your own lodgings beside the Arena, courtesy of yours truly and Agnes here. The money you boys reeled in was quite stunning and I needed something to spend it on so Agnes suggested this would be nice."

He was notably irritated at having to spend money on someone else and also for having to be nice to the boy that he would frequently beat and bully. But in his eye Luke could see that he had something planned, something malicious and evil.

"Let's go, Agnes, and leave him be."

"Is it okay if I stay and look at his wounds a bit longer? He doesn't look all that well to me but you go and I'll be back soon."

"No, you're coming with me, Agnes."

She grunted her disapproval and pushed him to the door rather forcibly. He twisted and caught her arm, looking as though he were about to hit her until he recollected himself and calmed down.

"Fine, have it your way but that means you're spending more time with me tomorrow."

"Yeah, sure, whatever," she quickly replied.

Luke had a feeling that Lamorte knew exactly what she was up to.

"How long?"

"Huh?" she responded.

"How long have I been out?"

"About ten days, so not long given your injuries."

"Is Kane okay?"

"Yeah, he's not bad, although you did break a couple of his ribs and he had a good helping of bruises from the Asian fighter. He'll live though."

"I bet he's upset that I had to save him though, eh?"

"Look, I haven't got a lot of time but once you're healed, you must wait for Kastas in your cell and he'll help you from there."

"What do you mean?"

"I can't say but I think he knows Luke, I think the Captain saw us that evening."

Luke cringed at the memory.

"He only kept you around for the tourney," she continued "But now that you've won and he's got his reward, he'll probably sell you to a much worse master. I don't want to see you hurt, Luke."

"What about Kane?"

"The Captain has no feud with him, so my guess is he'll keep him around to win more competitions. He's not that bad though, Luke, I know you've had bad run-ins with him but he's a good person, one of the best, I promise. Just trust me."

"He won't sell me, Agnes, he'll kill me! Surely you can see the malice inside him. For years, you've turned a blind eye on his actions towards us slaves, he whips us, tortures us and I don't even want to know what he does to poor Hal. He's a monster, why can't you accept that?"

He suddenly felt a cold pang of guilt at interrogating her like this but he wanted to know why she wouldn't believe him. Her rosy cheeks deepened in anger but it quickly dispersed and she broke down into tears. She pulled Luke close to her and between sobs whispered into his ear.

"Because…he's my father."

Luke let out an audible gasp as his eyes widened. For years, she had defended Lamorte, now he finally knew why and even though he hated the man, he was thankful that he'd looked after Agnes for all this time. For a moment, Luke thought of his own parents and how they will have missed him all these years. Now tears were welling up in his eyes but he quickly masked them when Agnes let go of him. Without uttering another word, she left.

Luke wanted to tell her how he felt but once again his tongue was tied. He opted to rest again and try to make sense of everything he'd just been told.

A few days had passed since Luke had last seen Agnes and he was no longer in the infirmary but in his damp and dingy cage. His back and chest wounds were now just scabs and his leg was no longer bleeding, although it was excruciating for him to move it too much. Kane had also healed well and was back to his arrogant self with his ego even bigger now that he had helped defeat the undefeated Asian champions. Neither of them talked of the event, however. It was a day they would rather forget as the pair of them had both stared death in the eyes and almost didn't live to tell the tale. The sun was just setting when Kastas came into the hall.

The old man was in a hurry and carrying a sword at his side which worried Luke quite deeply as the old man only carried weapons when he thought it necessary to use force instead of diplomacy. In his hands were two big rings of keys, one of which Luke knew had the key to his cage. As Kastas approached, he held his finger to his mouth as a signal for the boys to be silent and began to open the cage.

"The Captain doesn't look happy with you, Luke, so I'm getting you out of here. There are still many pirate crews here from the tournament and amongst them is Lu-Feng who happens to be pissed off beyond measure after you boys killed her best fighters. I was one of the reasons you are in captivity, Luke, and I'm so sorry for that my boy but I'm going to be the one to release you from it."

Luke didn't know what to say, he loved the man like his father and had never once blamed him for his capture. He settled for a thank you and followed him towards the stairs but the old man stopped at the foot of them. From his angle, Luke couldn't see what was going on but he could hear everything. Blocking them from escaping was one of Lamorte's crew, a middle-aged gentleman with a thick, pink scar running down the side of his neck. The two of them seemed to be having a normal conversation, so Luke assumed that the man hadn't seen him yet but wasn't going to wait for him to. Slowly, Luke crept back to his cage and shut the door, leaving it unlocked but making it look locked to anyone else's eyes. He sat down on his straw bed and waited for the man to walk down the rest of the stairs. *He must be tonight's guard. I can't go anywhere with him here.*

Luke wondered what to do next but it seemed Kastas didn't have the same worry, as the man came plummeting down the stairs with blood pouring out of his mouth and stomach. Just as the man hit the floor, Kastas drew his blade, which sent Luke into a panic. *If Kastas hadn't drawn his blade, then who killed the crew member?* Following the body was a short, almond-eyed pirate wielding two long daggers and shouting at Kastas. He wildly swung at the old man but the attack was blocked by his cutlass.

Luke ran out of his cage and grabbed a nearby broomstick to help his mentor with this unnamed foe. He drew near but Kastas kicked him away and threw his keys at him, commanding him to open the other cages. Luke was initially hesitant but Kastas was holding his own with ease, so he did what he said starting with Kane's cage and then making his way down the hall to open all the other cages. After the tourney, there weren't many fighters but a few had survived and there were those that were still training, so Luke had quite a few to open. By the time he had finished, there was a small army of them that all followed Luke to the stairs where Kastas had already finished off his attacker.

"Follow me," shouted Kastas.

He seemed to know what he was doing but Luke could tell that he was just as surprised at this turn of events as everyone else was.

They ran through the empty corridors of the Arena and walked out into the Pits to see the rest of the Arena engulfed in flames. Here and there were small skirmishes between pirates, all of them desperate to escape the inferno. Kastas led them through the armoury where they all picked up a weapon which they used to fend off the hordes of angry pirates that swarmed them as they left through the Arena's back gate. Luke, Kane and Kastas kept together and carved a path through the fighting towards the docks but they had a long way to run before they could reach a ship. Luke's leg was in agony and he ran with a limp but thankfully the wound had not re-opened, so he was able to continue towards the ships. As they grew nearer Luke turned to see the Captain's house also in flames, most of it turned to ash and cinder. *Agnes!*

Luke made a dash towards the house but Kastas grabbed him and hauled him back to the group that were fending off a few attackers, although most of the force were focussed on Lamorte's crew and any of his supporters. Luke turned angrily to Kastas, trying to fight away but the man's grip was a vice and Luke couldn't escape it. The old man looked at him dead in the eyes and told him to leave it be but Luke had to know if she was safe.

"Luke. There are others who care for her. Trust me, she's safe."

Luke knew that he was speaking the truth, the Captain wouldn't let anyone hurt her, so he agreed to continue on to the docks with their troupe of escapees.

They waded through bodies and conflicts, and after consistent running and fighting they made it to the docks that had thankfully not been touched with flame, at least not yet. Most of the boats were piling up with pirates also trying to run away from the conflict and destruction but Lamorte's flagship, the Oceanus only occupied three. Lamorte, Lu-Feng and Agnes. The two captains were locked in a vicious battle whilst Agnes looked on in terror. Fighting was rampant all across the docks but many of the pirates had alleviated their grievances and were now working together to escape the slaughter. Most of them stayed clear of the Oceanus and Lu-Feng's ship as that was where the combat was most fierce. Some of Lamorte's crew had planted themselves at the entrance to the Oceanus and were stopping anyone from approaching it; friend or foe, and the rest of the survivors had besieged Lu-Feng's ship and were advancing it, trying to wrangle control of it from her crew. Kastas was looking for a ship that they could use but they were all leaving their anchor points and sailing away from the chaos, so the effort was hopeless. In the end, Kastas decided that their best option was to try their luck with Lamorte's ship, so that was the group's next headed.

Luke, Kane and Kastas led the charge on the crew standing guard but thanks to their numbers, the fighters quickly overwhelmed the guard and filed onto the ship with Kastas leading them. He took them to the upper deck where they watched the ensuing fight between Lu-Feng and their master. Luke and Kane were keen to intervene but Kastas told them that it was only going to make the problem worse; the two pirate lords had to work it out for themselves, although none of them even knew what the problem was.

Agnes hadn't noticed them yet; she was too focussed on the battle that her father looked to be losing. She was powerless to help with no weapon. Luke felt sympathy for her but his own grievances with the Captain were too painful for him to ignore and secretly he wanted to be the one to kill him. Two of the fighters had been ordered by Kastas to lift anchor and unhooked the ship from the docks whilst he took the wheel and prepared to sail the ship out of port and away from any more of the two captains' respective crews who wanted to help their leader.

Luke and Kane, despite Kastas's disapproval, moved closer to the fight to try and understand what was happening and why, so they descended the stairs to the deck and hid behind them silently to listen in. Amidst the clashes of steel against steel was a stream of insults coming from the captains, with both of them trying to psychologically undermine their opponent.

"You are a fool, Lamorte, you chose to get rich and fat but that only made everyone else jealous. This was your own doing, your own greed and selfishness."

"I'd be careful, Lu, your skin is turning green."

"You killed my champions, so I will take everything you have. Well, everything that hasn't already burned down."

Lu-Feng was using a similar curved sword to that of her champion fighters, whereas Lamorte relied on his cutlass and long, curved knife that he used to deadly effect. Both of them were bleeding from an abundance of wounds but neither of them had yet delivered a finishing blow and were still ruthlessly attacking each other.

"You're too ambitious; my wealth is vast and will continue to grow long after I've killed you, so why don't you jump overboard and save me the effort of having to do it myself!"

"I've watched you get wealthier and wealthier, making flimsy alliances with those that would seek to destroy every pirate on this planet. I've been planning your downfall for quite some time, Lamorte, and I think it's time to show you what I've done with my time."

With that, the pirate lord stopped her onslaught of strikes and turned to the horizon. There, in the distance rose hundreds of ships, if not thousands, that were on their way to Lamorte's private sanctuary with the intent of destruction. Lamorte dropped his sword and sank to his knees in defeat, from the looks of things he had never seen a fleet so large in all his years of plunder and Luke was not surprised. The ships were beyond count, they filled the horizon and Luke had no doubt that there would be more.

"How?"

"Time, my darling. I had a lot of time and of course a good deal of money and wits, although I don't expect you understand that part. Pledge your service to me and maybe I won't kill you here and now."

Just as she finished her sentence, the ship departed from the docks and both captains turned their fierce gazes to Kastas. Luke took this distraction as a chance to end the conflict and with Kane he charged at the two captains, they were caught unawares by the two young men and that allowed Luke and Kane to push them apart and towards the sides of the ship. They were clearly outmatched by the trained fighters, so they were quickly disarmed and thrown overboard. Luke watched as they swam for shore and resumed their fighting but what he didn't expect was Agnes to dive in after them and go to help her father. If not for Kane, he would have done the same himself but his best friend convinced him that he wouldn't be able to help her if he was still a slave, which would have been the case if either of the captains had killed the other. All he could do was watch helplessly as hundreds of pirates rallied to their leader and swarmed each other. The Oceanus sailed away with Kastas as its new captain and ex slaves as its new crew.

Art Part 8

Art held his spear tightly as he approached the mountain with Kela flying high above him in her smallest form, no larger than a pea. Their morning had been spent training and planning, the same as the other six mornings since Art's escape, and he felt confident in his ability with the deadly weapon. Cold air rushed in with the rising of the sun making it the coldest morning Art had experienced on the island since he had arrived, which seemed like an age ago. They were heading to the secret entrance that Kela had found in the mountain to destroy the crystal that she said controlled the storm so that the island could be released from the curse that had been placed on it.

Since their reuniting, Kela had explained all she knew about the tribe and the storm, which was quite a substantial amount given that she had been living in a cave for well over what she thought was two hundred years, although Art didn't believe that she had lived that long. She had told him that the storm and its residents were relatively new and that before they worshipped it, the people of the island worshipped her, the sun and the moon. When the first storm rolled in, they had no idea what was happening, as tropical storms had never reached this size before, and they were massacred by the creatures that came with it. She said that it took a few storms for them to work out how to survive them but by that point there were very few islanders left. In order to survive, they had to regularly sacrifice lives to these monsters in return for their safety and protection. The sacrifices started as small creatures and then grew to become people and at one point they had even tried to sacrifice Kela, which was when she took her leave and made home in the cave with the crystals.

Then, after a few decades other people began coming to the island, travellers and merchants, who were welcomed by the people as saviours but slowly the islanders soured towards outsiders as they would pillage and plunder, deeming themselves more superior to the tribe, even taking them as slaves. This is what led them to become savage warriors and to attack any visiting boat, whether they were pirates or simple explorers. Once they had shunned foreigners, the storms became less frequent and the monsters granted them prolonged life if they sacrificed members of their own, which they began to do more and more violently. For many years, the people lived symbiotically with the monsters and did so far longer than any normal human but their sacrifices took a toll. They became savages, their society and social structures stopped advancing and so did their technology, leading them to become even more suspicious of outsiders who came with huge ships armed with firearms that would kill them with a single shot. At first, they were scared of this new technology and they fled from it, allowing many a lucky sailor to escape from the island and spread word of what they had seen. This is what birthed the tale of the fountain of youth, as many of the survivors came back to the island years and years later only to find that the tribe had not aged a day, and so more and more explorers and pirates tried their luck at obtaining eternal life or healing some sickness or other with the fountain of youth. Eventually the tribe grew accustomed to newer technology and before long they were able to slaughter any who ventured onto the island's shore.

That was as much as Kela could remember about the people of the island but the storm was still a mystery to her. She had no idea what it was or how it came to be but the story was invaluable to Art as it told him why the Captain had decided to risk coming here. He wanted to cure Art's mother with what he thought would be the fountain of youth but it ended up being his downfall. Art had long loved both Captain Lamorte and his mother but with one dead and the other chronically ill, he had no one left and that was why he needed Kela more than she realised, although he would never tell her. He preferred to keep his past quiet.

He trudged along, his back sticky with sweat due to the dampness of the air. It was hot and heavy, filled with moisture and the humidity wore on Art's spirits. His strength of both body and mind had improved greatly since arriving on the island but his heart was still weary with guilt and grief. Fear gnawed at him and his only escape from it was a slight slither of hope that held a beacon to the darkness and he used it as his secret weapon, his energy source and his willpower as he made his way towards the towering mountain and quite possibly the hardest challenge he would ever have to face. He was ready.

So far there had been no guards or scouts from the tribe, so Art's journey was unimpeded and peaceful, however when he got to where Kela had found the entrance he saw nothing other than a large, jagged cliff face. When Kela arrived, she seemed just as surprised as him to see her secret entrance had disappeared.

"But…'t was right here! Hang on a moment; let me check the area."

"All right but don't be long, this place gives me the creeps."

With that she made her way up to the cliff and inspected its surface with her tiny wings. She returned as quickly as she had left.

"It's hidden. But I think I know how to open it or at least reveal it."

"And?" Art replied impatiently.

"You need to say the password."

"I don't think yelling OPEN SESAME at a cliff is going to do much Kela."

"Don't get all sarcastic with me, Art, don't forget you owe me. Anyways, I agree that it sounds silly but when I saw it last, there was a human standing in front of it."

"So where's that human now?" Art asked whilst worriedly looking around him.

"Probably eaten."

"That's comforting."

"Just walk up to it at least and then I'll try and work out some sort of code, although I haven't spoken the tribe's language for quite some time."

Art slowly approached the mountain side and as soon as he got within a few feet of it, a small, round door appeared in a flash.

"Well, that was easy," muttered Kela, seemingly disappointed by the lack of effort required.

Art didn't feel like talking though, he wanted to get in and out before anyone noticed their presence. Leading up from the door that opened with a loud, crumbling creak was a long, steep staircase etched into the dark grey stone. Art looked up at the height of the staircase and was filled with dread. All of a sudden he was jealous of Kela's wings. She couldn't fly him however as she was keen on retaining her small size and to save her magic stores, so Art had to walk all the way to the top with his own two legs. It wasn't all that bad though, as a small breeze flowed through the cave from the abyss and mitigated some of the clinging heat of the tropical climate. Quietly they ascended the mountain's innards, up and up, until after a long time climbing they reached a huge cavern that must have sat right at the summit of the mountain. Inside it, all alone was a huge green jewel jutting out of a large stone pedestal, shining a beautiful viridian.

The two of them, sweaty and tired, entered the room and listened to its hum. It was an alien sound to their ears, cold and sharp but it had a calming quality that neither of them could quite explain. The sound made them forget their woes and replenished their hope but as they drew nearer to it they realised that they were not alone. Sprawled across the floor snoring, was an enormous creature with four spiny legs, a vicious tail and giant, gleaming fangs. To Art the creature seemed feline or fox-like but it was at least thrice the size of him end to end and most likely double his height with a snarling sneer on its face. Art held his breath and his knees began to wobble. This is what he had imagined the creatures from the storm to be like, except this one must be extraordinarily large as there was no way that another of its size could fit inside the cave that Art had hidden in.

Art looked to Kela who had stopped dead in her tracks and had landed next to the crystal but she had not seen the creature, instead she was focussed on the gleaming gemstone embedded into the mountain. Her eyes were wide and full of awe as she touched it and laid her head upon it to listen to its song. In victory, she yelled in a language that Art did not understand and leaped into the air. It was at that moment that she noticed the guardian of the cavern and she went from full of excitement to full of dismay as it stirred in its sleep and rolled about on the floor. Art held a bated breath as it changed position but to his bewilderment and delight it remained in slumber.

"Not very good at guarding things then," Kela whispered to Art with a snigger.

He gave her a look in response that shut her up quickly. This time she spoke in his head.

"Let's destroy that thing and then get out of here 'cause despite my previous actions, I do not want to wake that thing."

Art shivered at the voice as it rasped inside his head but he agreed with Kela and aimed his spear at the shimmering stone. With one strong lunge, he shattered it; the broken pieces falling to the floor in a great crash. He did not look to see if it had woken the beast, he just scampered back down the stairs with Kela on his tail but from the roar that echoed through the chasm he guessed that it had.

Agnes Part 7

Agnes was soaked through to her skin and pulled herself desperately out of the water and onto the rough wooden pier sticking out from the small make-shift harbour. She had swum the short distance from the boat to the shore faster than she thought possible to try and get to her father before Lu-Feng did. But she still wasn't quite fast enough and had to once again watch helplessly as her father fended for his life against the enraged pirate lord. The fires from the buildings were still blazing high into the sky, sending thick black smoke into the atmosphere but the collections of battles that had spread across the area were all but finished, with most of them ending with Lamorte's supporters fleeing from their opponents in an attempt to keep their lives and bodies intact. The last battle that echoed around the docks was between the two pirate lords but it was close to an end, as Lamorte's skill was wavering and his stamina depleting, leaving him open to attacks.

Tears flowed endlessly from Agnes's clear blue eyes as she screamed for her father's mercy, she even tried to run at Lu-Feng herself but her crew grabbed her before she got close. *What was all that training worth if I can't save those that I love?* She fought her captors' grip but they were too strong for her and she flopped in their arms in exhaustion, the fire within her slowly burning out. She watched as her father fell to his knees in front of Lu-Feng and begged for mercy but she didn't watch what came next, she couldn't bring herself to do it. She turned her head away and the men who had snatched her up led her away from the scene but her fire wasn't extinguished yet.

In one fluid motion, she broke free from one of their grips and hit the man in the groin, and then she spun and kicked the other man in the face, her flexibility surprising even herself, escaping his grasp as well. Her legs then propelled her away from them and sent her running into the wilderness. She didn't look back until she was well beyond their range of sight.

She couldn't see any pursuers but she still didn't feel safe, being alone in the wild with naught but her wits terrified her. Her eyes darted around for some sign of civilisation but she knew better than most that Lamorte's land was far from any other human settlement. *I have to go back.* The thought of returning was equally as frightening but it was her best option of survival. First she had to wait out the storm that Lu-Feng had brought with her.

Agnes's first decision was to find water, as her lips were dry and sore, so she began to search the area for some kind of potable source of water, as she was sure that heading to the river would make it too easy to spot her. Instead she remained where she was, as the high ground would make it impossible for the others to see her from a distance. And, after a short while of searching, she found a small, clear puddle of water. It wasn't the cleanest but it was the best she could do and it quenched her thirst well enough. She then decided to try and find some food, which she didn't have to travel far for, as a large bush full of berries had grown right next to the water.

They were sweet and juicy but not filling enough to satisfy her hunger. Since she had no foraging expertise or weapons, she had to make do.

When night set in, she settled in a large branched tree with a wide canopy of leaves that shielded her from both the cold and any unwanted gazes. She did not sleep that night but she did manage to find some comfort in knowing that Luke was far from there by now, sailing with his crew to somewhere he wouldn't be enslaved again. She didn't blame him for pushing her father off the ship, she knew that he was just trying to help but that didn't fix the fact that Lamorte was now dead and she was alone. There was not a thing that she wouldn't do to see Luke but she realised that their paths would not cross again, at least not for a long time. She vowed that she would do everything in her power to see him again.

Art Part 9

Art rushed out of the cavern almost falling over himself in his frantic dash for survival. Deafening roars were coming from the top of the mountain and were closing in on him at a frightening pace. The island was cold and dark as if it were night despite it being the middle of the day but Art was too preoccupied with fleeing the guardian beast's rage to realise that a wall of black clouds had surrounded the island. Art made a quick headline for the forest but a huge violent crash from the cliff said that he wouldn't make it before the monster had its jaws on him. His legs were tired and aching but they continued to speed on through the jungle, jumping over holes and fallen branches but it was to no avail. The monster was too fast, even the most steadfast of trees could not halt its pass as it ploughed through them and ripped them out of the ground. Eventually Art realised that he wasn't going to make it too far with his own devices.

"Kela, I need you to carry me and fly us to safety. I'm too slow to outrun this thing!"

Kela didn't reply but Art knew that she had some kind of plan and he was willing to rely on her. She swiftly paced ahead of him and bounced of a tree, propelling herself towards both Art and the beast. At first, Art thought she was going to try and fight the thing but he quickly realised that she was heading for him, not their adversary. Art braced himself for impact as she picked him up off the forest floor and continued along her path towards the monster with him clasped between her feet. They rushed past the beast inches from its mouth as it leaped into the air and tried to grab Art's dangling legs but it fell short and landed back down in humiliated fury. But it wasn't finished yet and it followed them from the ground below, its yellow eyes piercing through the darkness that had befallen the island.

Art watched it as it paced along, its back arching and folding to accommodate for its immense strides and its sharp tail trailing behind. From this height, Art could see how enormous it was. Its head extended past all but the tallest trees and its teeth looked like daggers jutting out from its jaws in neat, vicious rows, the canines dropping down to almost the bottom of its snout. It had scales rather than fur that glinted as it moved and spines where ears should have been but the most frightening of all its features was its head. It was adorned with spikes, scales and tufts of matted hair and right in the centre, on either side of its maw were two small, golden eyes with deep red pupils that had a ring of black around them to separate the two menacing colours from each other. The sight of it made Art squirm but that was not his only concern. Swarming around the sky were thick, sinister clouds arranged in a similar spiralling, hypnotic pattern as the storm but this was different, larger. The scale of it reached as far as Art could see and encompassed the entire island. Just as Art was about to speak the clouds let loose a downpour of rain and great gashes of lightning through the sky.

Through the mist, rain and darkness Art could see nothing but it seemed Kela could see perfectly fine through the haze, so Art trusted her instincts and just kept an eye out for the monster. Looking down, Art could just make out the image of the giant beast but around it were smaller forms, leaving the cover of the forest and joining the path that it carved through the jungle. It took Art a moment to work out that they were the creatures from the storm.

"Kela, what is happening? I thought we destroyed the crystal so that the storm wouldn't happen anymore!"

"Umm, yeah. So did I," she eventually replied. "I'm going to have to land, Art, this storm is making it hard to fly this high."

With that, she made for the mountain that stood indomitable against the weather, although Art could hardly see it and there they made a stand against the horde of creatures that were slowly emerging from the mist.

The rocks were slick from the rain but still sharp and cold and the crashes of lightning were constant, enveloping the island in bright white flashes that pierced the darkness. The great bursts of light were Art's only hope of seeing anything, so between them he was left blind and terrified. So far however he hadn't seen any of the monsters but their howls and roars still echoed to the top of the mountain's summit where Art and Kela were standing back to back.

After a few moments, Art and Kela could hear growls and teeth gnashing coming from just beyond the ridge. Instinctively Art clasped his spear tighter and readied it for a strike but the attack never came, instead there were a few agonised howls and screams from the creatures as a result of Kela's incantation. She had put up a magical barrier to protect the pair of them and anything that touched it would get zapped with its power but from the number of bodies jumping onto it and biting into it, it looked like it would not last very long at all. Then, after only a few flashes of lightning, it collapsed and with it came hundreds of rows of teeth.

Agnes Part 8

Agnes had spent three days in the wilderness, foraging for food and water but she decided that it was time to try and get back to the docks and find a ship to escape on. Smoke still rose from the Arena high into the sky but the fires had burned out, leaving the buildings in ruins. It saddened Agnes to see her home burned to cinders, and with her father dead and the Oceanus sailing far away she was both homeless and orphaned. To her, life had ended and there was no hope in bringing it back but she wasn't yet ready to die.

A huge expanse of tents and parasols had been set up around the docks where the entirety of Lu-Feng's fleet was docked. Agnes could see well over 200 ships and there were still more in the harbour, a testimony to the strength that the pirate lord had spent her life to achieve. Agnes was as close to the docks as she dared and was listening to the conversations between the pirates working around the far side of the tents where she was hiding behind a rock formation and some bushes. They spoke of plans to take control of the entire Western piracy operation, and with Lamorte out of the picture, they said it would be easy but Agnes was only focussed on finding a way out and that would only be by ship. Eventually the discourse evolved into them talking about the ships that had escaped the harbour before the fleet arrived and how only one of them had escaped. *Luke.* Agnes's heart froze; they made no mention of the ship's name or crew but she knew that Luke had gotten away; she trusted that Kastas would have led them away safely. Once the conversation had worked its way to a finish, the men moved away to continue their work elsewhere, which gave Agnes an opening to run into the rows of coloured tents and make her way unhindered to the docks.

Most of the tents, to Agnes's surprise, were empty, so she was able to advance quickly, only stopping once when a man left a tent to urinate, which he did on another tent, almost catching Agnes but she evaded his gaze and continued on once he'd left. The rows seemed to go for miles and by the time Agnes had escaped the labyrinth of coloured fabric she was completely worn out but she didn't have time to recuperate. She had to escape now or never.

Agnes was kneeling behind a dark blue tent that was empty inside bar from a small barrel and three beds and from there she watched and waited. There were hundreds and hundreds of pirates working and making merry around the docks, unpacking food and other valuables from the ships that filled the harbour. Some men were in chains and were being led to the Arena where Agnes guessed that they were being executed or caged but the majority were free and wore a strange symbol on their clothing, the same symbol Agnes had seen Lu-Feng wearing on the last day of the tournament. It was a ship's helm sticking out of the ground with a giant knife stuck through it as if it were holding it in place but around it were odd letters arranged in a circle. Agnes had never seen it before now but it gave her a sense of déjà vu and dread like it had caused her pain once before. Agnes chose to ignore it and before long was back to trying to find an escape.

She was certain that if she spent too long in one place she would get caught, so she moved from one tent to the other, weaving in between them silently like a thief but keeping her attention fixated on any opportunity that allowed her onto a ship. Many prisoners went by and most of them she didn't know but there were a few faces she recognised. Some were fellow crewmates, others were fighters and slaves, all dragged along the sandy path with thick clanking chains clasped to their wrists. She did want to help them but she was aware that doing so would get her captured which would be no help to anyone. She just had to painfully watch them get led to what she could only guess was their death or some other horrid fate that the pirates had decided for them.

After a few more minutes of waiting and lingering in the shadows, she found the perfect opening towards Lu-Feng's flagship that appeared to be preparing to leave. Agnes bolted towards the wooden jetty that it was messily tied to with a speed that she did not know she possessed and grabbed a back railing which let her push herself onto the empty deck. There were voices coming from below, which she assumed were the men stacking provisions and moving them to a safe location as there were crates and barrels full of food and liquor piled up on the deck. She grabbed a small barrel of water and threw that into one of the row-boats hanging off the edge of the ship, then went back and grabbed a handful of dried meats and fruits. After that she precariously leaped into the small boat just before the men walked up to the top deck. She was just about to cover the boat with a large brown sheet that had been left inside it before she saw the Oceanus, splintered and broken, docked up to the wooden jetty.

Aboard her father's ship were Kastas and Kane chained to the main mast with the entire rest of their crew's dead bodies scattered on the blood-stained wooden floor. Standing with a cold smile above them was a face she hadn't seen for a long time and hoped that she never would again. Clasping the wheel with an iron grip was Captain Krael, the man that had enslaved Luke and Kastas's old captain. She avoided his gaze and searched for Luke but she could not see him among the living or the dead.

Luke Part 9

Luke stepped off his rowboat onto the island's golden shores. He had been rowing for days after being pushed off the ship by Kastas when they had been boarded by Krael and his crew. He didn't want to flee; he wanted to fight the man that had ruined his life. He wanted revenge but inside he knew that the only way to do so would be to find help, so that was why he jumped into the small rowboat and rowed away from his friends against his heart's desire.

Luke knew that he wouldn't be trapped on the island for long as it was prone to sea traffic and was often used as a waypoint for tired sailors, which he had learned from Kastas. He first got out of the small splintery boat and pulled it to shore so that he had some way of getting off the island if it was necessary but after that he enjoyed his freedom. He breathed in a huge gulp of free air and dropped to the soft, warm sand. He listened to the waves crash gently upon the beach and the wind slowly rustle the trees, for the first time he could remember, he was free and it felt good. He wriggled his toes and fingers as if they were brand new and stretched out his body like it was his own once more. He wasn't completely free, however, as the nagging worry for his friends and Agnes stilled tugged at his mind endlessly and the wounds of his enslavement still ran deep.

Anxiousness stole away his feeling of euphoria and he jumped back up to his feet, searching for any sign of a ship approaching. To his disbelief there was one, it was small compared to other ships Luke had seen but it didn't appear to have any correlation with the huge fleet that Lu-Feng had amassed as it was coming from a different direction, so he counted his blessings and began to gather wood for a fire so that he could signal for help. He used some flint and a knife to start the fire, and as soon as sparks hit the dry coconut husks and sea grass it erupted in orange flame with thick smoke bellowing out of it. Luke looked to see if it had caught their attention, and sure enough the ship had turned and was sailing straight towards the island. He celebrated the small win and then sat back down on the beach to wait for their arrival but beside his right hand he left his dagger. He'd only had bad experiences with pirates and he wasn't going to trust these ones, even if they were on their way to help him. Or at least that's what he hoped.

By the time they approached the island, the sun was moving beyond the horizon but there were a couple hours of light still before the black of night. From what Luke could tell, they were a small crew of ten or so and only two of them came to shore. The two of them were smiling but Luke knew not to trust a smile by now and kept his guard up. Slowly they approached, stumbling over their own boots and merrily chanting an old sailors' song, clearly drunk. They first bowed to Luke, much lower than they could handle, as the pair of them lost balance and had to take a couple of steps to regain it, then they introduced themselves.

"Good evening. I am Josh and this is James, or Jim if you like. We're brothers. What can we do for you?" he shouted even though they were well within talking distance.

From the angle of the sun, Luke couldn't see them that well when they were walking up the beach but now he was able to get a good look and noticed that they weren't just brothers but twins, a rather awkward looking pair to say the least.

"I need safe passage to Tortuga, if that's okay."

"Not at all, my friend, join us. We were heading that way ourselves, although is it okay if we take that knife of yours? Don't want you slitting our throats as we sleep, do we?"

They both laughed hysterically at this comment but Luke did not see the humour, he was impressed that they had noticed the blade though. He handed them the dagger and followed them to their tiny rowboat, which looked too small to fit all three of them but they managed and together they rowed towards the ship.

"Oh, crikey! We've forgotten our manners, Jim!" he said to his brother before turning to Luke. "This is Jim or James if you like and I am Josh."

Luke didn't bother pointing out that they'd already told him, he just nodded and replied, "I am Luke, nice to meet you."

Their ship was in complete disrepair with scraps of rotting timber peeling away from the walls and deck and rusted nails sticking out all over the place but the sailors didn't seem to be too bothered by its flaws, in fact Luke guessed that they kept it in this state because they liked it that way. The rest of the crew were just as friendly as the two that Luke had already met and just as rugged if not more. Their smiles were missing teeth and their clothes were missing buttons but they were jolly all the same and Luke did not judge as he was sure that he looked much worse in his tattered, ill-fitting slave shirt and ripped trousers. The sun was setting as they sailed off towards the pirate paradise, cloaking the sea in a red aura making it look like an ocean of blood.

For the entire journey there, Luke had grown increasingly suspicious of the crew. He'd hardly ever caught them asleep or eating and when he did they would quickly stop and move away from him, waking instantly even if he was quiet. They weren't rude about it or suspicious themselves, they were as jolly as always, but it didn't sit right with Luke. Beyond that however, he found the voyage peaceful and he arrived at his destination in great time despite never seeing a map on board the ship but he was quick to leave their company, both because he wanted to save his friends and because of the crew's incredibly odd behaviour. When he departed from the ship, he waved a farewell and jogged up the steps to the small town, only looking back when he got the top because he'd forgotten his knife but the ship and its crew were nowhere to be seen. Luke turned back to his path and marched towards the closest tavern (of many). *No time for distractions, it's time to repay your debts to those that have risked life and limb for you.*

The inn was packed full of sailors, each one of them drunk as a skunk and failing miserably to attract the female bartenders with their slurred speech and inability to walk straight. Thankfully Luke did not recognise any faces but he kept as discrete as possible so as not to catch the attention of any who might know him from the gladiatorial fights. Luke however was not of any interest to the pirates and they continued with their own business without batting an eyelid, so he was able to sit down at a table and listen to the conversations being shouted from across one side of the room to the other.

"Can I get you anything, my dear?"

Luke hadn't seen the waitress coming and was so absorbed with collecting information that he practically leaped out of his skin at the sound of her voice. He turned to face her with a blank stare.

"Oh. I uh don't have any money, so not for me, thanks," he replied as politely as he could.

"That's all right, love, maybe go earn some gambling and then I'll give you a discounted jar o' rum, especially for the most handsomest customer here."

She winked at him as she finished and stroked his arm just before she left to deal with another table but she often looked back at Luke, which just made him uncomfortable. *Agnes does the same thing, what is it with girls and staring?* For a moment Luke forgot about his mission, distracted by thoughts of Agnes but he quickly regained focus and began to listen in once more.

Many conversations were about women and money but a few held pieces of information that Luke was able to put together to form some sort off a picture of how these men saw Lamorte. He wanted to make sure that they were all loyal to Lamorte and his reign as their pirate overlord in the West so that when he told them all of what Lu-Feng had done they would rally their own fleet and make war on hers, which would allow Luke to rescue Agnes, Kane, Kastas and the other slave fighters. So far he had realised that pirates had no loyalty except to their own captain and even that loyalty rested on the edge of a knife. It was time for him to get tactical about things.

Luke started by making his way to the loudest and largest table right in the centre of the room where he began to make conversation with a few men that were gambling there. His tactic was to try and steer the conversation towards how great Captain Lamorte was, which made him clench his teeth but he knew that it might be the only way to get through to them. They often shut him down and changed the topic of conversation to something more light hearted like their most recent kill or their favourite village to plunder but Luke wouldn't give up and eventually resorted to pulling out his trump card.

"I heard Captain Lamorte was dead at the hands of the Asian pirate lord," he shouted amidst a conversation about the tavern's food.

Luke was hoping that by saying it loud others would hear and join in but all he got were laughs from the men. A few however did look shocked and this sparked some conversations.

"By who did ya say, lad?" said an older gentlemen.

"Lu-Feng."

"Well, by the jolly roger, that's bad news. She'll be after us next boys!"

This garnered even more responses.

"What would she want with this stinkin' rat's hole?"

"This is the biggest pirate hub this side of Africa, I'd wager it's her next headed," shouted the old man.

Heads turned.

"I'll be damned if a woman takes my crew," yelled a voice from the corner of the room.

The entire building then erupted in shouts and arguments which eventually evolved into drinks smashing and brawls between huge clumps of men. Luke decided this was his cue to leave.

The brawls shook the tavern and poured outside where armed guards were standing in the street. They attempted to break up the huge row but it was all too large and they ended up being swept into it as well. Luke had no idea why they were even fighting, everybody seemed to be agreeing and acting civil but quickly Luke realised that the pirates were most likely just looking for an excuse to fight. He had to jump over a few unconscious bodies to escape but by the time he reached the other side of the street the fighting had fizzled out into small scuffles with a few men standing around the piles of unconscious bodies and injured men. Most of the armed guards recollected and began talking with the 'victors' who all pointed straight at Luke. His first instinct was to run but there was nowhere to go so he leaned on an unlit wooden lamppost and tried to play it cool.

The men did not speak a word until they were uncomfortably close to Luke with their swords drawn and aimed at him.

"You're going to have to come with us; we can't have ruckus-starting swine walking free around here. This is a civilised place, not your playground."

With that they grabbed both of his arms and tied them together painfully tight without even asking him his name. *Rules? In Tortuga? Are they being serious?* He was led through the town to the largest building there, which he guessed was the town hall, where he was taken down some flights of stairs and into a small, dingy cell not unlike the one he had been kept in for the last eight years. Luke argued and fought the guards' grip but they would have none of it and tossed him into the cell without another word.

"Please! I have to save my friends! They're trapped with the woman that killed Lamorte! Please, I need to help them as soon as possible!"

The guards laughed at his desperate cries and locked the cell, leaving the large, rusting keys dangling from a rack just opposite Luke. As soon as they were out of sight, he searched for a way out but with no windows and the keys to the door agonisingly out of his reach he could do naught but wait. He sat on the small, dirty bed and cried into his hands.

He had failed.

Agnes Part 9

Agnes had spent the last few days tied to a post in Lu-Feng's private tent after being captured on the flagship. With ample amounts of water and food, she felt as if she were some royal guest and she had been treated as such. The pirate lord spent much of her time talking to Agnes and asking her for advice on things that Agnes didn't even understand but no matter how much she asked, Agnes was never told about the whereabouts of her friends. Lu-Feng would tease her with information but she never gave an explicit answer leading Agnes to speculate that they had been executed along with most of the other captured men.

The first ropes that Agnes was tied up with she managed to bite through, making her captors swap them for impregnable steel chains that chafed her skin and dug into her wrists and ankles. Without a key, they would be impossible to escape from, so Agnes had begun digging at the ground to try and loosen the metal pole she was attached to and thanks to the fact that Lu-Feng and her guards had not entered the tent for a day or two, she had made good progress. Her hands were bruised and bleeding from a myriad of wounds from her desperate digging but she never gave in to the pain.

Night had caught up with Agnes and before long she was completely exhausted and rested her eyes during a break from digging. When she opened them, however, streams of light were flooding in from an open flap in the tent and silhouetting the figure of the pirate lord herself. She was smiling jovially, an odd sight on her usually cold face but her body showed a completely different image as in her hand was a decapitated head and the blood of the victim had stained her entire body from head to toe like she had hacked it off herself. Agnes tried to move so that she could see who the head had belonged to but the light was too intense.

"I'm afraid I have had to execute another prisoner today, my dear, I can't have any mutiny from my workers, can I? You'll forgive me if I place it by your side, just to show you what happens to those who disobey me." She then leaned in close and whispered in Agnes's ear, "That means stop digging."

Agnes took in a gulp of air in shock as the mutilated head was placed in front of her. The face was initially turned away from her but it slowly rolled over to reveal a pale, haggard face with a crooked nose dripping blood and a pair of old brown eyes. Staring back at her was Kastas's sweet peaceful face.

"Nooooooo!!!"

Agnes kicked the head away in a bout of fury and turned her face away from it. Her cries echoed through the rows of tents and sent birds fluttering away from the posts they had been perching on.

"Yes, I had a feeling that he was a friend of yours. I'm very sorry, Agnes."

"No, you're not! You knew that he was close to me!"

170

"I wouldn't dream of hurting you, my dear."

"Well, that's all I dream about!"

In a fit of rage, Agnes jumped to her feet and ripped the pole out of the ground. Before anyone had a chance to react, Agnes was swinging it around her head, aiming at Lu-Feng. The ensuing crunch of the pole hitting the pirate lord's face was enough to make Agnes gag and the blood that spurted out of the wound completely drenched one of the tents walls, making the room glow red. Agnes then dived through the open tent flap and sped towards a boat that was just leaving the docks. Lu-Feng's guards were too busy to warn anyone about Agnes's flight and by the time they left the tent in search of her she had disappeared.

The men on the boat she had leaped onto did not notice the stowaway that had hidden herself between barrels on the lower deck. Before she knew it, they had disembarked from the dock and were sailing away from Lu-Feng.

When the crew walked past, Agnes would hold her breath so as not to be caught but at night and during the early hours of the morning she would leave her hiding spot and carefully scavenge the ship, which one night led her deep into its bowels where she found a transport of prisoners with Kane amongst them. They would talk for a few moments but they were always careful to remain quiet. However, it was enough for them to catch up on everything that had happened, including Kastas's death, which brought fresh tears to Agnes's face and turned Kane's usually colourful face pale and sullen. Eventually they talked through a to re-take the ship.

The plan started with Agnes finding out where they were headed, which was easy enough as after being lubricated with alcohol, the pirates would talk unnecessarily loudly, unintentionally telling Agnes that they were a prisoner transport headed to Tortuga to make a quick profit from their slaves. Next, Agnes was to find the keys to unlock the cage that the ten or so prisoners were being held in and pass it through the bars to Kane. Once she had done that, she grabbed a handful of weapons from a room stacked full of them and stealthily took them to the prisoners along with some food and water which they lapped up greedily. The last part of the plan was the hardest but with Kane leading the assault, the pirates surrendered quickly without too much bloodshed. There were very few sailors left, so the rest were stripped and thrown overboard at Kane's request as he knew that they would rat the slaves out as soon as they stepped foot on dry land no matter what promise they made to Agnes. After only a couple days of planning, the ship was theirs.

All of the prisoners, including Agnes, changed clothes into those of the pirates so that when they arrived at Tortuga they looked the part and weren't questioned. One of the prisoners was a captain of a crew, so he took the wheel and directed them all towards Tortuga whilst everyone else manned the sails. They had become quite close, even if they had only been prisoners for Lu-Feng for a few days and they all without question opted for Kane to be their leader with Agnes as his right hand woman. Thankfully the air stayed sweet and the weather was calm, so they found themselves on the shore of the pirate island in no time.

The wind was quiet and cold there, threatening a storm and the air grew salty and sharp, which Agnes took as a bad omen. Only she and Kane were left on the island, the others had sailed off, hoping to abuse their freedom but Kane and

Agnes wanted to find any sign of Luke they could. When Kane had told Agnes that Luke wasn't dead, she was ecstatic but slowly she began to feel the same dread as before because no matter whom they asked, no one had seen him. They had tried every tavern except for one and that was where they were going next.

The timber was old and crooked, so much so that Agnes doubted its safety and most of the tiles on the roof had fallen off and smashed onto the paths below but the atmosphere inside was totally different. Everyone was making merry and laughing, which made Agnes's nerves settle a bit, although she wouldn't have trusted a single one of those sea dogs if her life depended on it; they were still vagabonds and thieves and murderers with little decency.

The sun beamed through the glossy windows into the rooms, illuminating all of the awry faces and missing teeth but it was not warm to the touch. The two of them began by talking to one of the barmaids.

"Excuse me," Kane began "Have you seen a young man around here, around the same age as us? He has skin like hers and is quite broad in the shoulders."

"What's it to you?"

"Everything," Agnes replied.

The barmaid looked her up and down in disgust and then turned to Kane with a synthetic smile.

"There was a man with that description 'round here not three weeks ago, quite the handsome one too."

Agnes fought the urge to hit the girl, and Kane, feeling the tension, held her arm back.

"Do you know where he is now?" he asked.

"He was taken to the prison in town hall for starting a bar fight."

"Thank you," Kane responded.

He then reached into his pocket and pulled out some coins.

"For your trouble," he said.

The two of them then paced out of the tavern and made their way to the town hall.

The trip was short but full of suspicious stares from the locals. At first, Agnes put it down to them never seeing a black man with a white girl before but now she wasn't so sure. The townspeople had the same ominous feeling as the air around them which Agnes had never known in Tortuga; usually it was such a pretty place full of life. When the two of them reached the town hall, Agnes realised what they were worried about. It was the symbol sewn into the jackets they had taken, the same one that Lu-Feng wore around her neck. Then it dawned on Agnes, the last time she had seen this symbol was the day her mother was killed.

Art Part 10

Lightning cackled in the distance. Hundreds of the monsters came leaping at the two lone fighters, teeth gnashing and snarling as they drew dangerously close. Art levelled his spear at the first one that came bounding up to him and it skewered itself with the sheer speed it was travelling but the next one was close behind.

"Kela, help," he yelled, the panic seeping into his voice.

His companion however was busy fending off her own foes to help Art. Laboriously he struggled against one of the beasts, his spear within its jaws and his entire force pushing against it. It wasn't enough, however, and he had to pull back the spear and plunge it into the exposed belly of the creature, the spear's wings stopping it from punching a hole all the way through it and out the other end. With a yelp, the monster fell off the end of the weapon, its limp body resting awry on the cold stone floor but Art had no time to celebrate as another three monsters had appeared in front of him. The rain was torrential and made the scales on the monsters slick and slimy as well as the sharp rocks that jutted out of the ground. Art continued to fight off the beasts through the downpour but eventually he was surrounded.

Before Art were piles of dead monsters that he had felled but for every one he killed, two more appeared until they had encircled him and driven him back so that he was now back to back with Kela who was also being overwhelmed. The monsters could see their distress and slowed their attack, their long, spiny tails swinging side to side and their jaws imitating a smile. They were playing with their food.

"Kela? Any more tricks?"

"Nope, all out!" she returned as the beasts slowly prowled towards them.

But just as Art was about to give in, a huge deafening roar shook the mountainside. Art audibly gulped and held his spear, drenched in thick yellow blood, close to his chest, his knees almost buckling with fear but he stood his ground. The advancing monsters seemed just as scared of the behemoth and also moved back, some even turning and finding a perch to watch the ensuing bloodshed but Art and Kela had nowhere to go.

"I figured it out," shouted Kela, surprisingly excited.

"Not a good time, we need to think of something or we're dead!"

"The crystal! It didn't cause the storm, it regulated it and so by destroying it, we've trapped the island in a cycle of endless storms!"

Art only listened partially to her, as he was much too busy watching the colossal monster predatorily amble towards them with its tail in the air and its teeth bared.

"Art, you need to run back to the cave you found me in."

"What!" Art nervously cried back, worried by Kela's serious tone.

"When you get there, you'll see a crystal at the bottom of the lake, the only one that does not shine any colour. Once you have it, you're going to run to the hall where we destroyed the other crystal. On that pedestal, you must place it and then get out of there as quick as possible."

By now, the monster had joined its smaller counterparts and was watching the two of them with its beady yellow eyes, enjoying their pain.

"But what about you?"

"I think I know what to do." She smiled. "Now go! And don't look back!"

Art turned, spear in hand and ran for a small jagged path down the mountain. To his surprise none of the monsters followed him but thanks to the rain the path was slippery and unstable with small rocks falling down the cliff as he ran by. When he got to the edge, he began to descend but just as his head went below the line of rocks, Kela began shouting.

"I haven't done this for an age," she roared.

Art spent no time waiting around and as he looked up, he could see Kela's shadow flash into the sky, illuminated by a bolt of white lightning and larger than life. *She's changed size!* Art suddenly grew less worried for Kela and hurried down the cliff incredibly swiftly, rarely losing his footing and only slipping when he got to the ground. When he got there, however, he had no clue where to find the cave entrance but he knew that wasting time would be deadly, so he started to trace the wall for the opening, much like he had done the first storm but with much higher stakes. His hand was cut and slashed by the sharp rock but he pushed through. In a moment of carelessness, Art's spear slipped from his grip in the darkness and fell down a huge, black hole in the ground. Art was tempted to pursue it but he did not want get stuck as that could be more lethal than not having the weapon at all. However, as he looked around, he realised the surrounding trees were familiar. This was the hole that Kela had flown him out of and without further questioning, Art dived in.

He rolled about through the tunnels, speeding down towards the cave and hitting the walls as he went. Eventually the tunnel led out into the cave below where Art came crashing down, landing with a splash into the cold underground lake. The icy water shocked his body and for a moment he forgot where he was but the crystals glowing in the darkness below quickly snapped him out of his confusion and he began searching for the colourless crystal amidst the green and pink glows of the iridescent stones. And, sure enough at the bottom of the lake was a grey crystal, void of all colour or glow, however, it was deeper than Art thought he could swim. He considered his options but given that they were limited, he just ducked his head under the water and swam down. The descent felt slow and painful, like wading through thick mud and the deeper he went, the worse it got until he felt like his chest was being compressed by a huge weight that pushed all the air out of him but that wasn't going to stop him and he continued swimming down. *Just keep swimming.* Thanks to the glow of the crystals, he could see clearly and when he opened his eyes, the grey crystal was staring right back at him. Art then grabbed it, expecting some resistance but it came freely and he was able to push off the lake floor and ascend back to the claustrophobic air of the cavern with the large gemstone in his hand.

He took a giant gulp of air as soon as his head broke the water and he threw himself onto a rocky ledge jutting out from the side of the lake where lay down panting profusely. He held the crystal above him and watched as it began to pulse with a black light that absorbed all other light around it but it was calming, much like the other crystals. It tempted him to stay and rest but he knew that there was no time, so he jumped back onto his feet in a burst of elegant agility and picked up his spear that was absently floating in the water. From there, he made his way to the entrance to the cave, suddenly remembering that it was an impassable, slippery incline.

Art approached the ramp and began to climb but hardly made it two metres before sliding back down, so he tried again this time getting further. He slowly but surely continued onwards until once again he lost his grip and was sent tumbling back down, which considerably dampened his spirits. Small gusts of cold, fresh air came flowing through the tunnel, teasing Art to try again but he realised it was hopeless, especially when he realised that the path was blocked by the stone that had killed the first monster he came across. Art resorted to thinking of a plan, which he did whilst staring at the now dark grey crystal. At first, art thought it was just the crystal that was pulsing with a dark light but as he turned towards the cave wall he saw that it too was flashing, not as bright but in time with the crystal. Without any other ideas Art moved carefully towards the wall and began pushing on it but it would not budge, the only change was that now the whole wall wasn't flashing, just a thin black line in the shape of a curved door. Art squinted his eyes and tilted his head in confusion but slowly a new idea began to formulate in his mind. Following his instinct Art traced the line with the crystal and as he finished the last part, the stone gave way and opened, revealing the outside world.

The tranquillity of the cave made Art forget how ferocious the storm had become but now that he was back in it he realised just how powerful it was. The wind pushed him back and the rain battered against his skin and the lightning continued flashing ceaselessly in the sky. Art sluggishly made his way out of the door and into the forest through the onslaught of the weather and as he looked back, the door closed. It took a moment for him to realise but the door was in the same place as the door to the stairs that led up to the cavern in the summit of the mountain. *It's like the stone knew where I wanted to go.* Art turned it over in his hand with a new wonder in his eyes and then walked back towards the cliff, hoping that the door would open. The door once again did just that and Art was free to ascend the steps but just as he made his way up the first set, a roar caught his attention. At the entrance were three large monsters, their maws drenched in dark red blood.

Art readied his spear and placed the stone on the floor all in the same movement and the beasts came hurtling up the stairs in single file, the passage too narrow for more than one at a time. Art took this blessing with a thankful heart. The first jumped straight at Art and was easy pickings with the spear; however, the second was more careful and advanced at a much slower pace, always keeping its eyes on the point of the spear. In a spurt of courage, Art decided to charge first which caught the creature off guard and he was able to skewer it right between the eyes, leaving the third monster alone. This creature made the charge first but leaped straight over Art's head and scraped his vulnerable back with its razor sharp claws which sent him tumbling down the stairs in a heap. It then turned its attention to the stone whilst Art ascended the stairs to continue the fight. It was curious about the crystal and prowled around it a few times before plucking up the bravery to touch it. However, as soon as its scaly paw touched the stone it was instantly vapourised, the dust quickly blown away by the wind up the cavern. *I can't do anything on my own, I'm weak! Every situation I find myself in, I need help! I thought I was doing well for a moment there, for a second I was strong and independent. What went wrong?* The thought ate at Art but he tried his best to continue onwards.

The injury on his back had slowed him down, the blood dripping down his leg and down into the abyss below with some of it seeping into the murky stone steps like a thick red ribbon following Art's limping path. He hoped beyond all things that he would be in time to save Kela but given that he'd been gone for a while, he was unsure if she'd still be alive.

By the time he reached the top of the stairs, he was drenched in blood, sweat and rain and exhausted but he dug out the strength to pull himself to the pedestal. As soon as he got close to it, the crystal began to glow a bright white light and it seemed to magnetise towards it so that when he let it go it was pulled straight onto the pedestal. It stuck there hovering over the thick, black stone letting off a hum similar to that of the other crystal that was now shattered on the floor. This song however was very different. Where the other one was calming, this one was off-putting and uncomfortable to listen to, however as the song went on it changed into something much more smooth and elegant. As soon as this change happened a thin bolt of lightning burst through the chamber and struck the crystal with such unstoppable force that Art thought it would shatter it but instead the stone looked as though it was absorbing the bolt and dragging the storm with it.

Cold air suddenly flowed in through the chamber and so did the rain, all falling into the crystal that had now changed from white to a dark blue and when the clouds began to be absorbed into it, the stone began to glow a deep, swirling purple with bright white dots of light speckled within it like the stars. Art watched as the stone took in the violent storm with ease, settling it and changing the sky from a purple-black to its usual sunny blue but the chamber was still filled with the swarming mass of thick black clouds that hadn't yet been taken in by the crystal. After a few seconds, they too were taken up. Within a few moments, the storm had been appeased.

Art wiped his brow and collapsed heavily onto the floor, his eyes still focused on the crystal. At first, it looked steadfast but slowly cracks began to show on its shimmering surface and they slowly spread like a web until the crystal looked like it was about to implode. Finally, the surface broke and chunks of crystal burst outwards in a flash of light, some sinking deep into Art's skin. Following the explosion, the sky went black as if the storm had been released once more but only for a second as the darkness was taken in once again by the heart of the crystal that exploded just as the last wisp of darkness was absorbed. Art watched the unfolding events in horror and then relief but eventually his body gave way and he no longer had the strength to keep his eyes open.

Luke Part 10

Early morning dew dripped off the mould-covered windowsill and Luke tried his best to lap it up as he had hardly drunk anything since being locked up in the cage which from what Luke could guess was around three weeks ago. But the captivity felt much longer than that. The only sight of sunlight he got each day was in the late evening when the setting sun would beam its orange light through the small, barred window and the only fresh air he was allowed was also from the small window through the thick wall. At night, the cage would be freezing and during the day it would roast him but in the morning it was mild enough for him to enjoy it without feeling like he was being scorched. He thought that his heat tolerance would have increased substantially over his eight years in Africa but when he was trapped in a room with no purpose or entertainment it was abysmal. Most of the time he spent keeping up his strength by using his body-weight as a resistance, pulling himself up with a thick, iron bar that stuck out of the wall above his bed and doing press-ups as well as jumping and squatting, however the rest of his time was spent resting. After constant slavery and imprisonment, he had given up.

Many a thought lingered on his friends and their safety but with no motivation or remaining will-power Luke was helpless and felt weak like he once had when he was a boy on Krael's ship. More than ever Luke wanted his revenge on that man, it was the only thing that gave him enough strength to wake up each day but it wasn't enough to make him want to escape. Luke was more than tempted to let his troubles fade away and his body rot in the damp, dingy cell.

After having his fill of water, Luke went back to the bed and sat on the end of it watching his cage door. For the first time in a while, he heard commotion from the guard room that wasn't caused by alcohol but he could not pick out what the voices were saying and didn't recognise them either. He sat like this for hours, just thinking and listening to his fellow prisoners. One of them that he'd grown especially close to was an older gentleman with a harsh, quiet voice and a keenness for animalistic noises but despite his shortcomings he was kind towards Luke and empathised with him whereas most of the other prisoners at best ignored him and at worst mocked him. The old man would often offer advice to Luke and comfort him but mostly he talked about what he would do when he left the prison after his ten years locked up in it.

"You know, Luke, the first thing I'm gonna do is strip stark naked and jump into the sea. I miss her."

"Take soap then, 'cause you stink like a dead man," replied Luke with a little laugh.

"I don't know, I've grown quite fond of the stench beneath my pits."

They both laughed at this sarcastic response, which made Luke feel much better.

"What about you, my lad? What will you do?"

"I don't know. Probably find myself behind bars in some other place."

"That's no way to think. You're young but less fun than my father and he's dead! Come on. There must be some lady out there?"

"There is. Was."

"And?"

"We were good friends but I ruined it and now I don't know if she's alive or dead."

"Oh, sorry I asked," answered the old man quite bluntly.

"What's that supposed to mean?"

"Well, like I said before, you're less fun than a cemetery. But I won't push. What did she look like?"

"Her eyes were like the sea, blue but much lighter, purer. And when she smiled, everyone would turn to stare, you couldn't look away. Although I think that's because you pirates aren't the most accustomed to the smile of a woman."

The old man giggled at this.

"I'm offended but also impressed. You made a joke, Luke, a bad one but it's progress!"

Luke ignored him and carried on speaking, lost in his memory.

"Her hair was brown, dark, but when the sun hit it, it would shimmer and effervesce like a gemstone. But what I loved most was her fire, her determination to grow stronger so that she could protect those dear to her. She's stronger than me. Much stronger."

In that moment, the guard room door swung open and out of it fell one of the guards, his nose bleeding and his arm clutching his gonads. Following him was a familiar face holding a wooden staff.

"What a coincidence," shouted the old man. "She looks just like the woman you had described, Luke! Luke?"

It took him a few seconds to realise.

"Oh," he finally whispered.

Luke stood staring at Agnes and she returned his longing gaze. Both were motionless, Luke grabbing his cage bars and Agnes holding onto her staff. Even the other prisoners were silent as the two lovers reunited with each other. Agnes was first to move and ran full speed to Luke's bars, grabbing his head through the bars and kissing him. In return, Luke put his hands on her hips and pulled her even closer. Her lips were warm and tasted sweet like honey and her hair smelled like blossoming flowers. Dripping down her cheek were salty tears that Luke wiped away with his fingertips. They both then opened their eyes and continued gazing until Agnes broke away and grabbed the keys off the wall, opening the cage with the first key she tried and pushed open the door to greet Luke with a warming embrace.

"Follow me," she calmly whispered in his ear whilst pulling him out of the cage into the hallway and through the thick, iron-clad door into the guardroom.

On the way past, Luke grabbed a sword and continued following Agnes into the main hall of the building where Kane was busy fending off two other townsmen. Luke joined the fray quickly and together the Taijitu bested the guards, taking their weapons and throwing them into a nearby room that was then promptly locked with five tied-up guards inside. When Luke got outside, however, their advance was halted as the sun was too much for his eyes to bear, so Kane and Agnes had to fight a couple more men to allow Luke time to accommodate to the bright yellow, solar rays. As soon as he did though they were back on the move and advancing at pace through the main market square of the pirate town. Here they met more cheers than resistance as the pirates were pleased to see the local officials take a beating.

The three of them made their way to the docks and labyrinth of jetties to find a boat but when they got there they were greeted by a host of unfriendly faces baring arms and one face in a particularly foul mood. *Lu-Feng.*

"You know this place isn't too bad," she shouted. "Although it doesn't even come close to Madripoor. Oh, well, I suppose as the overlord of piracy I'm going to have to get used to slums like this."

She then proceeded to walk up to the trio, taking her time on the steps and dragging her sword along the path as she drew near so that it made an abhorrent screeching sound which sent shivers down Luke's spine. By now, they had racked up quite an audience where almost all those nearby had come to watch, and Lu-Feng took this opportunity to introduce herself.

"I suppose most of you will be wondering who I am and why I'm here. It's quite simple actually. I killed Lamorte, so that makes me the pirate queen and you my subjects. Any objections will be treated with…hostility. For years, I was shunned and mocked just for being a woman in a world where men seem to run everything, so I have decided to change that. Starting from now, you will pay homage to me and know that I am the ruler of the seas!"

She then turned to Agnes, hand held out.

"Come on, darling, join me."

Agnes Part 10

Agnes froze. She didn't know what she was expecting but it wasn't that. The scar from where Agnes had hit Lu-Feng was still raw on her face and yet she offered her hand. Agnes was about to respond but a man stepped out from behind Lu-Feng, his right arm missing.

"Please, Agnes. Take the offer, she's a great woman, you just haven't seen what the future can be with her."

"Hal? Why would you betray the Captain?"

"Agnes, Lamorte was a bad man, surely you knew that? Just ask Luke and Kane and anyone else that he saw as inferior. He was a tyrant. The world is better off without him."

"Not my world," Agnes muttered under her breath.

"So?" interrupted Lu-Feng. "What say you?"

"If I agree, can you promise my friends will be safe?"

"I promise."

Agnes turned to face Luke and made to join the pirate queen but Luke grabbed her hand and shook his head.

"You can't trust her. Don't worry about our safety, we can handle ourselves. Right, Kane?"

"Don't you know it," he replied with his usual arrogance.

"Please, Agnes. Find somewhere safe away from here, away from her."

"I wouldn't listen to him, Agnes; he clearly doesn't want what's best for you. Like all men, he wants you for his own selfish, lustful reasons but I want you to join me and rule an empire. Just us women, against the whole world. You know that it's the best decision."

"No. I will not forsake my friends. If you want me, come and get me but I'm sure your face remembers how well that went last time!"

Lu-Feng groped the long, pink scar on her face, her eyes misting red in rage and unsheathed her long, curved blade.

"Leave her to me. The others are to do as you please!"

The men surrounding her smiled maliciously and licked their lips before charging at the trio with weapons drawn.

Lu-Feng led the charge, her eyes never leaving Agnes who stood above her at the top of the stairs, awaiting the clash of steel against her hardwood staff. The first strike was easy to dodge and the second was easy to block but as Lu-Feng fell into rhythm the hits became harder and faster until Agnes had to retreat back up the path behind her. Luke and Kane had their hands full with at least half a dozen men each and the rest of the crew Lu-Feng had brought along were desperate to join the fray. Agnes knew the further back she retreated, the more Luke and Kane would be surrounded, so she made an attempt to push forward, battering her adversary with huge swings but she was stubborn and held her ground.

"This brings me back," Lu-Feng mumbled out of the blue.

Agnes continued thrusting at her but was visibly confused by the comment.

"20 years, Agnes. Am I right in saying that?"

Agnes stepped back, eyes wide in realisation. The charm around Lu-Feng's neck was swinging as she slashed with her sword and in that moment memories of Agnes's mother flooded into her mind but it was too much handle and she fell to her knees with the staff held above her head in defence.

"What?"

"YOU HEARD ME," the enraged pirate screamed, hacking down on Agnes's weapon after each word.

Suddenly the staff snapped into two equal sections, leaving Agnes exposed but Lu-Feng stepped back and wiped her brow instead of administering the final blow.

"I wasn't there but I heard of the…accident. Such a pity too, I was rather fond of your mother."

A single, solitary tear trickled down Agnes's cheek and dripped off her chin onto the floor. Agnes was instantly filled with a rage-inflicted strength and she bore down on Lu-Feng with such immense strikes that she had to fall back. Agnes took the time to see how Luke and Kane were doing and to her amazement standing with them were other pirates, those that were loyal to Lamorte, fighting off the growing threat of Lu-Feng's enormous crews. The pirate queen herself seemed just as surprised, as her eyes were wide and for the first time Agnes had witnessed, she looked scared.

"What was that you said about an empire?" Agnes smiled.

She then continued her assault on the woman, hacking and slashing and spinning as Lu-Feng tried desperately to stop the onslaught but her courage had failed and the strength she once had was diminished. Where one piece of the staff would deflect, the other would attack in a blur of motion and Agnes quickly overpowered her. In a last attempt to fight back, Lu-Feng lunged at her but the younger woman grabbed her arms, hit it with one of her staff pieces and snatched the curved sword from out of her hands. Agnes without thinking then raised her arms and hit Lu-Feng square in the face. Blood spurted out of her nose and within seconds she was on the floor unconscious from the blow Agnes had inflicted with the other staff segment.

Agnes wasted no time in joining Luke and Kane in their fight. The three of them fought back-to-back and piled up bodies around them, mostly injured or unconscious but some were killed in the action. Luke would often finish off an enemy for Agnes and she returned the favour just as much but Kane was pretty much left to his devices, although he didn't mind and from the look of things help wasn't necessary. He was like lightning flying from one strike to another, leaving his enemies in the dust and swirling through their attacks like quicksilver, whereas Luke was steadfast and strong, unmoving like a mountain in a storm. His blows shattered swords and broke bones with hordes of men falling before him. Agnes felt like she was a mix of the two of them. Here attacks were fluid and swift but she preferred to hold her ground and let her enemies come to her, and she was just as effective as either of the other two. In the chaos, Agnes forgot about Lu-Feng and when she looked where the woman had fallen, she was missing, which worried Agnes deeply. She frantically spun and searched whilst also fighting a particularly strong pirate but by the time she had spotted her it was too late and her blade was sunk into Luke's hip. He fell to one knee but continued fighting the men directly in front of him with no time to turn and stop Lu-Feng's next strike. She lifted her curved sword high above her head and sent it plummeting towards his neck.

Time froze as Agnes watched in despair. Other men pushed those fighting Luke back, so the brute of a man was able turn just in time to see the blade sink into the man that had pushed his way between him and the steel blade. He had salt and pepper hair with a ragged beard and a haggard frame but Agnes knew who it was in an instant. He turned and smiled at Agnes one last time as his body collapsed to the ground limp, the life slowly draining from his dark blue eyes. She let out a blood-curdling scream and ran for Lu-Feng and in a vengeful swing her staff connected with the woman's neck sending a crack echoing through the docks. Agnes watched as her eyes rolled back into her head and she fell back into Hal's outstretched arms. Both his and Agnes's screams could be heard throughout the island.

Eventually the chaos came to a standstill and those that had supported Lamorte chased off the last of Lu-Feng's crew back to their ships but Agnes was too involved with caring for her father.

"Hang on, you'll be okay! You just need some help!" she cried whilst stroking his cheek. "Quick, Kane, go get some help!"

She divided her attention between Luke and Lamorte who were both bleeding heavily into the paved floor. She was aided by a local who tended to Luke as she looked after her father. Kane came back with the town's medic, but he could do nothing, the life was already leaving his old body.

"Quick! Do something to help him! Please!"

Kane spoke in the doctor's place.

"Agnes, he's…"

"He'll be fine, just help him!"

She knew that it was hopeless but she didn't want to lose her father again. For a moment, her eyes drifted to Luke who now had the doctor's care and then fell back to her father's.

"Please, don't go. Not again."

"I've done terrible things, Agnes," he croakily responded. "I think it's best you let me go. You've made me so happy. I want to die with those memories but always remember them. For me."

"I will, Captain."

Her tears were falling onto his chest as she laid her head down on it in one final embrace but she tried her best to smile for his sake.

"I've done horrible things to Luke. I hope he can forgive me and that you two can spend a happy life together. Although you might want to teach him romance as from what I saw that evening, he's not very good at it."

He laughed at his little joke and then closed his eyes.

"I thought you'd seen that," Agnes whispered but she knew that he couldn't hear her.

Tears flooded down her face and she continued to hold him but she soon moved to Luke and cared for him. He and Kane were now her last family; she wasn't going to let them die any time soon.

His injuries weren't the worst she'd seen on him, as Lu-Feng's chop at his side had been stopped by his hip bone and the other cuts and scratches were shallow, so wouldn't cause him much problem. However, Agnes took the opportunity to fuss over him and milk his injuries so that she could spend extra time holding him and tending to his wounds. He also seemed pleased with the attention. Every time she went to see him he had a huge smile plastered onto his face and it would not fade until she left his company.

After about a week, Luke was in much better condition and could walk, so she would take him on little journeys around the island, which went much better than their first romantic encounter, especially since they now both knew they had feelings for each other. Initially Agnes slept in a different room in the inn but eventually she began to spend the night with Luke in his room, which was amazing other than the looks she got from the waitress that clearly had eyes for Luke with his blonde hair and rippling muscles. Money was a small problem but Kane managed to rake in heaps of gold coins from arm wrestling the drunken pirates in the tavern, so for a while they were well set and could enjoy the time on Tortuga but the pain of her father's passing was often too much to bear and she spent many lonely hours thinking about him and mourning his death. When around three weeks had passed, Agnes felt it was time to leave and Luke concurred but Kane had grown quite fond of his money-making schemes, so getting him to agree proved to be quite the chore. Promises of his family were what convinced him and the three of them went in search of a captain.

Lots of buccaneers had visited the island to pay homage to the late pirate lord, so they had a huge range to choose from. On the third day of their search, they found themselves drinking tankards in the largest tavern on the island with the wealthiest captain, Gregor.

"Lamorte was by far the worst pirate I had ever met," shouted the man. "Me and 'im were quite the pair when we were young though, always trying to get rich with the most outlandish scandals! You should have seen us; we were young, handsome and ambitious!"

Hearing about her father made Agnes realise how secret he had been about his past and how much she truly missed him.

"How did you three get to know him?"

Kane and Luke looked at each other and smiled.

"Old friends," they said in unison with a little giggle.

"What about you, my dear?"

Agnes wasn't sure what to say but finally she found the words and was proud to say them.

"I am his daughter."

"Illegitimate, I guess!" Gregor laughed.

But then his expression changed from humorous to deep in thought.

"But then that would make you the heir to his estate. And in turn that makes you the Pirate Lord of the Western hemisphere! My dear, you don't need a captain, you need a crew!"

Agnes was taken aback by this revelation. All her life she though she wouldn't amount to anything in the pirate world, so it took a moment to set in and for her to fully understand what this meant. At first, she pictured herself as a monarch, respected and revered but then images of Lu-Feng's tyranny flooded her mind and the prospect became much less intriguing. Her mind fell into turmoil at whether to accept the fact or refuse but before long she made her decision.

"I don't know what to say. I would love to but…"

Then Luke grabbed her hand, tenderly kissed her cheek and spoke for her.

"A crew would be quite nice." He smiled.

She mimicked his smile and stared into his eyes before turning to Gregor who was also beaming bright.

"It would be nice but I do not wish to do it alone," she stated. "I want Kane and Luke to help me."

"You're in charge, so I suppose that is the way it is then. Three pirate lords. I think this could be interesting!"

Art Part 11

Birds chirped jovially as the sun dressed the trees in an auburn glow and the waves gently crashed against the shoreline. It took a moment for Art to come to his senses. *Is this what Heaven is like?* The island looked the same as it always had but tranquil and picturesque. His body couldn't move at all except for his eyes but he was sat up on a rock near to where he had placed the crystal. He quickly realised that was completely alone. Suddenly, like a weight lifted off his chest, Art could move the rest of his body. His breaths were long and deep as he smelled the fresh air with no hint of malice or fear, no hint of the storm. In an instant, memories overflowed Art's mind. He began to remember all that had happened up until the moment that he thought he'd died. To some extent he hoped that he were dead because that would mean that the reason Kela wasn't around was because she was alive, a comforting thought for Art to dwell on. However he still felt the sharp twangs of pain in his body, a feeling that he was told Heaven would take away, so his better judgement said that he was still alive, against all odds.

With this Art got up, ignoring the dull ache in his head, and began to search the area for Kela in hopes that he would find her alive and not a carcass half eaten by monsters. Thanks to the summit of the mountain being blown clean off by the crystal's explosion it was easy to climb to where the two of them had faced off against the horde but try as he might, he could not spot Kela. To him this was somewhat good news and his hope was renewed so he continued with a new strength. It was flapping wings that ended his search.

Hovering above his head was Kela with a monstrously proud smile, back to her normal size and happy as ever.

"I got you some water."

Art was too busy to notice before but his mouth and lips were parched and his stomach was empty, so he lapped up the water greedily.

"What happened?" he finally asked.

"Oh a little lightning, rain. You know, storm stuff."

"Please, Kela, my head hurts already."

"Oh, you're no fun! Basically the crystal that we destroyed regulated the storm rather than controlling it, so by destroying it we made an eternal storm and angered the big mama of monsters. When I saw the crystal, I was reminded of the one that I asked you to replace it with, as they had similar magical auras and thankfully that crystal was strong enough to destroy the storm, although I don't know how."

"That's comforting."

"Well, I created it, so if anything else happens, I'll know what to do. I think."

"That doesn't help much but go on."

"Oh well, I went supersized when you left and pretty much decimated the local monster problem and then went looking for you. I don't want to alarm you but you were dead when I found you."

Art was unfazed by the information.

"You not bothered by that?"

"I'm way too tired to bother with that now, maybe I'll freak out later instead."

"Good plan. But what was it like?"

"I can't remember it really, all I can remember was darkness and…"

Art fell to his knees in realisation and remembrance.

"And?" she inquired.

Art wanted to answer but his mind had begun to replay the events and he was living it all again.

At first, there was a white light, a silhouette with gold around the edges against a bleak, black landscape and a deep voice. Art knew it instantly. *Captain Lamorte*…tears rolled down his rosy cheeks and he ran towards the man. Their embrace was tight and loving.

"I thought you were dead?"

"Dead? I suppose that is the technical term but within you a part of me lives on."

Art didn't understand what he was saying, at first he thought he was referring to Art's memory of him but the sentiment was deeper than that, more real.

"What do you mean?"

"I think you know, Art. I think you've known for a while now."

Then in a flash the image was gone and Kela was staring blankly at him.

"I'm not sure I healed you properly. Life is difficult to recreate, so who can blame me?"

"I saw him, Kela. I saw my father."

"I suppose that was what your heart truly wanted you to see, that was why you were able to come back to life. Your mission is not quite over."

"No. You're right. I still need to save my mother."

"I could help with that but my wings are a bit too tired for a flight like that. We need a boat."

Art was once again full of vigour, a welcome change to his usually weak will and body.

"Then let's go find one!"

Together they made their way to the stairs.

"What is her name by the way? Your mother."

"Agnes, Agnes Lamorte."

Luke Part 11

Agnes had been offered a small but sturdy ship and four crewmen from Captain Gregor in return for a promise to repay him once she acquired an empire and gratefully she accepted. Luke was confused as to why she would want to give him and Kane a portion of her power as she was the one that had earned it but as long as he was with her he was happy and being able to share freedom with Kane was an amazing bonus. They had talked for years about what they would do with endless liberties but neither of them thought the day would come when their chains would be removed. However the moment was sad, as they wished to share the time with Kastas but Lu-Feng brought his life to a short end, a life they could not bring back however much they mourned his passing.

The sun was rising on the horizon, its warm amber rays illuminating the ocean and washing their face with a golden glow. The three of them were sitting in the crow's nest of their new ship, Luke in the middle with Agne's head resting gently on his broad shoulder and Kane's arm on the other. The three of them in unison inhaled a deep, rejuvenating breath and watched the clouds as they slowly drifted away towards the sun. Birds tweeted and cawed in the tall trees and butterflies danced on the bright petals of the blooming flowers, slurping up the sweet nectar inside. A slight breeze tickled their cheeks and the air smelled fresh and new with a hint of the salty sea. Despite all they had been put through, they had found peace and unity in the chaos and they loved every moment of it.

"What now?" asked Kane who had already tried to relinquish his part of being Pirate Lord.

"I suppose we set sail. Adventure will find us, I have no doubt," replied Luke whilst softly stroking Agnes's hair.

"I would like to see my family, my old life."

"So would I, but we're pirates now, wanted criminals. Wherever we go, trouble will follow and I don't think I want to get my family mixed up in that. My family is here now; I don't need to dwell on what I thought I had lost when I have gained so much," responded Luke.

Agnes pulled Luke closer and kissed his hand.

"I think it's time to re-write our stories," she whispered.

Luke looked thoughtfully into her eyes and then turned to Kane before staring into the horizon.

"Plus, I have a grudge to settle."